GREG

THE SETTLER BOOK ONE

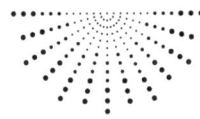

KATHLEEN BALL

Copyright © 2018 by Kathleen Ball

All rights reserved.

No part of this book may be reproduced in any form or by any electronic or mechanical means, including information storage and retrieval systems, without written permission from the author, except for the use of brief quotations in a book review.

❦ Created with Vellum

I dedicate this book to all the readers in my facebook Kathleen Ball Western Romance Readers Group. If you haven't joined feel free to do so https://www.facebook.com/groups/1343221899115875/ . I appreciate each of you.
And as always I dedicate this book to Bruce, Steven, Colt, Clara, Emery and Mavis because I love them.

CHAPTER ONE

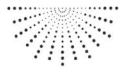

At the loud crack of a rifle shot and the subsequent bullet whizzing by his head, Greg Settler dove for the ground. He'd barely lifted his head when another shot rang out, kicking up the dirt next to him.

Jumping Jehoshaphat! What was going on? He'd finally arrived in California and drove his pickaxe into the ground to stake his claim. Not a minute later he was waiting for death. He'd heard the Goldmines of California were dangerous but he hadn't imagined anything like the situation he was in now. Afraid to move, he crouched behind a bush, his mind raced for a solution.

"I'll cover you! Make a run over here!" A voice to his right called out. "Ready? One, two, three, run!!"

Greg had never gotten up and sprinted faster in his life. He dove into the dark cave-like opening in the mountain, gulping for air. "Thank you."

A few more shots were exchanged before all was quiet. He glanced around the beginnings of a shaft mine. The front was shored up with lumber and it served as this man's living quarters too.

The man quickly put out the oil lamp and sat in the dark shadow keeping watch across the stream.

Greg sat up and leaned back against the side of the shaft. "What was that all about?"

The man turned toward Greg. Only he wasn't a man at all, and Greg's breath caught with his surprise. Although it was dark, he could make out her features. She was quite pretty with bow-shaped lips and long blond hair. He couldn't tell the color of her eyes. For some reason, that bothered him.

"It's simple really, someone wants your claim." Her voice flowed like honey, and he wondered how he'd ever mistaken her for a man.

"I haven't even started it."

"You drove your pickaxe into the soil. You started it all right. I'm just glad I was here to help. My pa went for supplies, and I'm guarding our claim. It wasn't necessary a month ago, but some color was found a couple claims down and now everyone thinks this place has gold on the ground ripe for picking. They'll turn this area into another boomtown and bring all its problems with it."

"I'm Greg Settler from Oregon." He put out his hand.

She wiped her palm on her pants before accepting his handshake. "I'm Mercy Watkins. You'll find out soon enough that you can never seem to be mud-free out here."

Greg smiled. "Been out here long?"

"If it's not one claim it's another. My pa has gold fever. We've been at it since March of 1849. We make enough to keep us fed."

He cocked his brow. "It would seem like a female—"

"Don't say it. I'm a hard worker, and there's nowhere else I'd rather be," she said in a defensive tone.

"I'm sorry. No insult intended. I have two sisters, Scarlett and Cindy. Both hard workers, but boy does Scarlett love her dresses. Cindy is more of a homebody, but... I'm not saying it right. My pa has a way with words, not me. It's admirable that you are a hard worker and helping your pa."

Her laugh was smooth like a fine Kentucky whiskey. "No harm done. I'm used to men telling me to go find a husband and a home to live in. To me this is my home."

She put down the heavy canvas flaps that covered the front of the mine and then lit the lamp. "I've got coffee and bread if you'd like some."

Greg swallowed hard. She had the greenest eyes he'd ever seen. She was beautiful in the lamplight. Her honeyed blond hair curled as it spilled down her back. She was also covered in dried mud. People told her to marry? She appeared too young to get married.

"Much obliged. I have some food and supplies on my claim, but I suppose it isn't safe to be on it at the moment."

"That's why you need to sit by the door with my rifle and keep watch over your things." She handed him the rife and the bullets. "My pa will whistle three times so don't shoot him by accident."

Greg loaded the rifle and took up post at the front of the claim. He was off to the side and had a good view between the flaps. "Does this mean I won't be sleeping ever?"

Mercy handed him a cup of coffee and she placed a tin plate of bread next to him. "It's best to have a partner. I guess you have gold fever too."

"It would be nice to earn my fortune, but I really just wanted to do something that was my own. I want to build something and make something of my life."

She glanced at him. "They threw you out of the house, did they?"

He furrowed his brow. "They most certainly did not. In fact tears were involved when I left."

"Hope you had a bandanna to mop up your face as you rode away." She laughed her whiskey laugh again.

"I come from a family made up of orphans from the Oregon Trail. Our ma and pa taught us to think for ourselves and make something of ourselves. We live on a big ranch, and I could have stayed but I wanted to try something different. Restless feet, I guess."

"A big family sounds really nice." He could hear the longing in her voice.

Three short whistles from outside interrupted them.

"Pa's home."

A large man with wide shoulders pushed through the flaps with a large crate in his hands. He dropped the crate and reached for his gun.

"Pa, don't. This is our new neighbor, Greg Settler. He was being shot at, so I took pity on him."

Her pa looked Greg up and down before he nodded and took his hand off the butt of his gun. "I'm Hugo. It's nice to meet you. You've never mined before, have ya?"

"Nice to meet you sir, and no I haven't."

"Just call me Hugo. We don't go by ceremony around here. Mercy probably told you someone struck gold nearby. Now we have all kinds wandering about. We can take turns keeping watch tonight, and tomorrow we'll get your tent up. You did bring a tent, didn't you?"

Greg turned his attention to guarding his mine. "I certainly did and probably a lot of useless stuff. They recommend everything at the supply store in Hang Town."

"Where's your horse or did you come by boat and then walk?" Hugo questioned.

Greg didn't take his eyes off his claim. "I traded my horse for a mule."

Mercy laughed so loud that Greg glanced her way and saw her shoulders shaking hard.

"What?"

"Your horse was probably worth ten times what Ole Blue is worth," Hugo said in amusement.

"Ole Blue? How'd you know the name of my mule?" Greg was getting tired of being laughed at.

"Ole Blue is traded to new miners. Usually to the ones the stable owner, Hank, thinks will quit fast. They always bring him back the mule and Hanks trades the same mule to the next new miner. Don't worry. Ole Blue is a good mule." Hugo rummaged through the crate. "I can add a can of beans to your bread if you like."

"That's mighty good of you." Greg had found that refusing this far West was the same as an insult. He shifted his attention back outside, glad to have the distraction of watching his claim or he'd probably be staring at Mercy. Hugo probably wouldn't take kindly to that.

In short order, they ate, and Mercy made two pallets on the benches inside the mine. One on each wall.

"I'll take first watch," she offered. She walked to him and took the rifle from his hands. "My bed is the one on the right. Take it and sleep."

He was about to reject her offer when Hugo stood up and stretched. "Get to bed, boy. Mercy is good at guard duty. She won't fall asleep on the job."

"Make sure you wake me—"

"Don't you worry. You'll get your turn," Mercy interrupted. "Scoot so I can sit there and keep an eye on your things."

"What about Ole Blue?"

"She's been in camps longer than anyone. She knows to care for herself. Now, good night." Mercy stared at him until he got up. Then she promptly sat down and ignored both men.

Dawn approached, and Mercy woke as she did every morning, before the sun. It was still cold this early in the spring season. She wrapped a blanket around her shoulders and started a fire. Next, she put a big pot of coffee on to boil and almost laughed at how deeply the lookout was sleeping.

Greg sure was a handsome man. His hair was nut brown. The color of an acorn, she mused. He sported a well-trimmed beard. He didn't have the hardened look of a miner yet. There were still smiles left inside of him. His broad shoulders would be a help to him. He didn't smell as bad as the rest, yet, either.

He'd be safe once the sun was up. No one would shoot in the morning hours. There were too many people around. Did he know the dangers that faced him out here? He didn't look too green. There were callouses on his hands, so he wasn't a milk toast miner. His teeth weren't black or missing, so he wasn't a man who paid no mind toward caring for himself.

His eyes opened, and he caught her staring. Her face heated as she quickly turned away.

"I guess I fell asleep." He scrambled to his feet and quickly pulled the flap back then sighed in relief. "My things are all still there."

Her lips twitched into a smile. "You got lucky. Remind me to never ask you to guard me." She couldn't help but tease him.

Greg smiled back, warming her. "Well, I wouldn't blame you. I don't have a proven record here yet."

His eyes matched his smile which was unusual among the miners, except for the ones who struck it big.

After she poured some coffee, she handed it to him. "We'll

have our coffee and then get your tent set up. After that you start digging. Am I going too fast for you? You look lost."

"Not at all. I'm just absorbing everything you're saying. At what angle do I dig?"

He tilted his head as though he thought she wouldn't have the answer. "A hard forty-five degrees and as wide as ours is. Then you'll want to dig in a straight line. You'll need lumber in a few days or so."

"You're quite knowledgeable for a... I'm sorry. I'm going to have to get used to the fact you know more than me and you're female."

"Female she is, and keep your mitts to yourself or I'll have to shoot you," Hugo said from his bunk.

"How many have you had to shoot already?" Greg asked.

"None."

Mercy shook her head. "Only because I chase them away before he gets a chance. A man who wants to court me will arrive with flowers someday."

"Go on, the two of ya. Get the tent up, and Greg, you let Mercy show you where to dig. She's usually pretty lucky at picking a spot."

Mercy put on a gun belt, checked her pistol for bullets and then grabbed her hat and coat before stepping out into the cold morning air. Her breath made little white puffs as she pulled on her coat. Work would warm her up.

She walked over to Greg's claim. Well, Greg had missed a person pulling his stake out of the ground. Men! She picked up the pickaxe and turned in a circle for all to see and then she sank it back into the ground. She tipped her hat to the small audience that had gathered.

"Listen up. There was shooting last night over this here claim. It's been claimed, so no more shooting if you know what's good for you." She pulled her coat back enough to expose her gun. "I don't know where a lot of you are from, but here we stick to the code of no stealing from a miner and no claim jumping." A few men narrowed their eyes at her and a few smiled. The others just shook their heads. She stood there until Greg joined her. By then most of the men were gone.

"They respect you." There was a sense of awe on Greg's face.

"Of course they do. Like I told you, I'm a hard worker, and that's what is respected most out here." She patted her holster. "That and my gun. Now don't listen to any rumors of me shooting a man in the head. I mean, I shot at his head, but I only got his ear."

Greg laughed. "What?"

"He came into the mine and tried to have his way with me and ended up running away with only half an ear. Oh my stars, talk about a lot of blood!"

She frowned. "Why do you stare at me like that, Greg? You would have shot anyone who came into your claim and put his hands on you!"

Greg stopped looking so amused. "You're right I would have. Glad he didn't hurt you. Is he still in camp?"

"My pa would have killed him if he hadn't skedaddled."

Mercy pulled a tent out from his pile of belongings. "Let's get started. I have a mine of my own to tend to."

She'd shocked him. She could tell by the look on his face. She wanted to laugh, but she put on her poker face. She didn't need another miner to think they were meant to be together. It got irksome, and one of these days her pa was going to have to up and kill one of them. She tried everything she could to discourage the men. With Greg, she was having fun at his expense. He actually seemed to be a good man, though time would tell.

"I do know how to put the tent up, you know," Greg grabbed the polls and followed her.

GREG

Mercy stepped back and looked at their handy work. "It'll stay up. Stop over if you need anything else."

"Wait, where am I supposed to dig?"

"Inside the tent for now."

His brow furrowed.

"Look, start on the left side and put the dirt on the back right side. You don't want anyone to see what might be on the piece of land. If you find gold keep your mouth closed about it. What you are actually doing is carving out the mouth and living quarters of your mine. Dig down and out toward the opening to your tent. You'll want to be able to walk into your mine. Make it as big as mine and then shore it up with lumber. Then you dig your shaft into the earth. I'll stop by later to see how you're doing."

"Thank you, Mercy. You've been a great help."

Her face grew warm. "Well, it will be nice to have a normal person next to us for a change. There's food at Ima's tent. It's over yonder. Most eat there, and in turns. You watch someone's claim and then they watch yours. Got it?"

"I got it."

"See you later, then."

GREG ADMIRED her as she walked away. She was so different from the women back home. Heck, she couldn't be any older than fifteen or sixteen, yet she had an air of confidence about her. But if she was so lucky picking the digging place, then why were they still trying to find gold after all these years? Or maybe they'd found it and Hugo gambled it away?

Greg had seen a lot of that in Hang Town. In fact, he'd seen an awful lot more in that mining town. But at least there were buildings there. Here, the town consisted of a big muddy street with mostly tents serving as businesses, the largest being the saloon. He'd peeked in and got more than an eyeful and left. He'd never seen women in such state of undress. Weren't they cold?

He'd seen men in expensive suits buying mining gear mixing in with the miners dressed in rags. Gold fever hit all kinds. He saw riches to be made besides gold. Lumber mills, supplies, homemade food were gold mines of their own. First he'd try his hand at mining.

Picking up his spade, he dug and dug. He was glad of Mercy's advice. He had thought he'd just dig here and there or pan for gold even. But the streams were played out, and a lot of the surface dirt had been gone through. The only thing left was going into the earth.

"Hey, Greg, It's Hugo," called out his neighbor. "Don't shoot."

Greg leaned heavily on the shovel and waited for Hugo to come in.

Hugo whistled. "By golly. You work fast. You'll want to grade the front a bit. If it rains you don't want the water sloshing into your mine. Come take a look at ours after the noon meal. That's why I'm here, to take you with me."

Greg looked down at his dirty clothes. "I'll need to change."

Hugo laughed. "You look cleaner than most. Come on you'll see. Ima makes the best pie this side of the Rocky Mountains. Now, you can pay by the day, but she'd rather be paid by the week. Sometimes miners forget to eat and she doesn't think she should be out of money for food she cooked and they missed. She's a nice gal. Keep your hands off her."

Greg nodded as they trekked down the hill to a big tent. He spotted Ima and she was no gal. She looked to be old as dirt. Maybe to Hugo she was still young. She rushed over to meet Greg. She wore trousers and she was as skinny as a starved rabbit.

"Howdy do?" She stuck out her hand and Greg shook it.

"No spitting, go light on the cussin' and wait your turn. Those are the rules. I'll make up more as needed. How'll you be paying?"

"By the week, ma'am."

Ima smiled brightly. "Good idea. Seeing as it's Thursday and I collect money on Saturday I'll only charge you for half a week."

Greg started to protest, but Hugo stuck his elbow against Greg's ribs.

"Sounds fair to me." He dug into his pocket, took out some cash and handed it to her. He expected some change but he wasn't offered any.

"Go ahead and go through the chow line. You only get to go through once so pile up your plates—except for dessert. That you can have only one of. Coffee is on each table. If you bring your own tin cup and plate, I give a discount. Enjoy your meal."

She hurried around to the other side of the table that held the food and doled out the mashed potatoes while making small talk with each man. Greg watched as most piled meat five or six pieces high, leaving room for not much more. Hugo roared in laughter and Greg turned to see what was going on. Ima was hitting a man with her spoon.

"You scoundrel! That plate is bigger than any of the others. No cheating. You get this one warning, then it's cold cans of beans for you! Put some of that meat back then go eat." She muttered under her breath as she shook her head. She shook her head so hard her braids of gray hair shook back and forth too.

THE TABLES WERE MADE of long planks of wood, the seats roughhewn benches that resembled sawhorses. Greg nodded at the group of men who sat at the table Hugo led him to. They all quickly looked away. *Friendly crowd.*

"Boys, this here is Greg. He has his claim next to mine. Funny thing, someone was shooting at him last night. Did any of you see anything?" Hugo put his tray down and sat.

Greg did the same as he glanced from one man to another. No one looked the least bit guilty. They were all different shapes and sizes, but all he saw was the caked mud on their faces. It was going to take a bit to figure out who was who.

Hugo took a big bit of ham and began to introduce the others to Greg. "That one there is Smitz, then Mac, Glad, and Longster."

"Nice to meet you."

They grunted and continued to eat.

"Don't you want to know why they call me Glad?" asked a tall, stocky man.

"Because you're pleasant?"

Everyone at the table laughed except for Glad.

"It's short for Gladiator." Glad seemed to be waiting for some response, but Greg wasn't sure what.

"That's very interesting."

"Just don't get in my way," Glad warned in a gruff tone.

Greg nodded. Was he given that name or had he made it up to sound tough?

"I heard the shots, rifle shots last night," Smitz said, his voice low and soft. "They came from up high on the opposite hill."

"Someone opened their flap about gold being here and now we have all the riffraff coming in."

Greg thought of his ma. She'd consider the men at the table riffraff.

GREG

"I'm taking him under my wing," Hugo announced.

Each man gave Hugo a solemn nod like it was some code of the miners. Whatever it was, Greg was grateful.

"Did you meet Mercy yet?" The man named Mac asked. Mac had two front gold teeth and from what Greg could tell they were the only teeth he had.

Greg chewed his food before answering. "Yes I did. She's a lovely person, and she helped me tremendously."

"Saved your bacon, did she?" Longster asked.

"She sure did."

They finished eating and headed back.

"You looked for gold while you were digging didn't you?" Hugo asked.

"Of course I did."

Hugo nodded. "Good. Next thing is to put the dirt outside of the tent so you have somewhere to lay your head.

Greg looked at him.

"The sides of the tents roll up. Just shove the dirt to the outside. This will serve two purposes. One you have room in the tent. Two, people see that you didn't find anything and will hopefully leave you be for a while. Keep your gun handy at night and keep you lamp low. You don't want to make yourself a target. In another day or so you can move your tent to the side and start shoring up your entrance. Come on to my mine. I'll show you what I mean about grading."

They walked through the flaps to Hugo's mine and both men quickly turned their backs toward Mercy. She'd been changing her shirt and she didn't wear undergarments. Greg didn't see much, but he got the impression of creamy soft skin, and he caught the slightest glimpse of her curves.

"Pa, you're supposed to whistle. You can turn around now. I'm clothed."

Greg figured she'd be the one blushing but it was he who felt heat on his cheeks. "Sorry about that, Mercy."

"No harm done." She gave him one of her warm smiles. "How's the digging going? Are you rich yet?"

"Fine and no. I'm here to see about grading to avoid flooding."

Mercy began to explain how it was done while Hugo went into the mine with his pickaxe. Greg listened to her in fascination. She sounded more like an engineer than a miner.

"You're educated."

"You noticed?"

"You know boys don't like smart girls, at least that's what my sister Scarlett says."

"I don't care, never did. I'm too smart for that kind of logic."

Greg laughed. "I do think we can be good friends, Mercy."

"As long as you don't try to get too friendly we'll do quite well together. Now scoot. I have a mine to work."

"Yes, ma'am." Greg wanted to smile as he walked back to his tent, but he put on his best expressionless face. Happiness usually equaled a gold strike around here, and he didn't want to put himself or Mercy in danger.

All he thought of while he shoveled the dirt out of his tent was Mercy. She was so unlike anyone he'd ever met, her presence in mining country so unexpected. But mining for gold was just the adventure he'd been looking for.

"Well, hello good looking."

Greg startled, grabbed his gun, and spun around. Standing inside his tent was a beautiful blond woman with not nearly enough clothes on. He swallowed hard, not knowing exactly where to look.

"Hello, ma'am."

She laughed. "Your ma must have taught you some nice manners. My name is Shelly. I just wanted to say hello. I like to greet all the new men."

"Nice to meet you. I'm Greg Settler. Are you in camp with your husband?"

"Aren't you a young one. Unjaded, I like that. No I work in the saloon tent. I was hoping I'd see you there later. The first one is free."

His jaw dropped and his face heated. "Excuse me?"

She fluttered her eyelashes at him and gave him a coy smile. "The first drink, silly."

"Would you like to put my coat on? It doesn't seem—"

"I put on an extra petticoat for the walk over. I'm fine. I usually don't make house calls but in your case I could make an exception." She walked closer with each word until she had her hand on his cheek. "I'd like us to be friends."

He took a step back. "A person can never have too many friends. Listen Shelly, I need to get back to work, but it was nice to meet you."

She frowned and looked around his mine. "Maybe you wouldn't be able to afford me. Have you found any gold yet?"

"Not yet but one can hope."

CHAPTER TWO

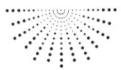

"Will you stop pacing? You're making my head spin," Hugo told Mercy.

"She's been in his tent for a long time, don't you think?" She frowned and then peeked out at Greg's tent again.

"No, not too awfully long. I bet they are just jawing." He didn't sound very convincing.

"You really believe that? I don't even know why I'm the least bit perturbed. I mean he's a man after all. Men have needs. I hear it all the time."

"You hear too much and see too much out here in the camps, and I'm sorry for it."

"No use fretting, Pa. You know there's nowhere I'd rather be." She shrugged. "I just thought he was different is all. But a man is a man. Shelly is so pretty, and she knows how to talk to a man. She has sweet words to say, and I don't know any. Maybe I should ask her to teach me—"

"You will not. You do know what Shelly is. You'll end up like her, and your days of misery will start and stay with you. We'll make a big strike, and then we can have a big house on the hill."

"Yes, Pa." He always dreamed of the big strike they'd have. They had more than enough gold already, but he never saw it that way.

A flash of color drew her gaze outside in time to see Shelly ducking out of Greg Settler's tent. "Finally! She's making her way down the hill. I'll be right back."

"Mercy, where are you going? What do you plan to say to him? Let the young man be."

She put her hands on her hips but held her tongue. Her pa was right. What was there to say? She might not want to hear anything that came out of Greg's mouth anyway. He might have wonderful feelings about the half-dressed Shelly. Glancing down at her own mud-caked pants, Mercy sighed. She'd end up an old maid miner. Or worse, she'd end up with a toothless man with dirt in his veins. She wrinkled her nose at the thought.

"How old do you think Greg is?" she asked.

"He's seventeen. I asked him. I'm not sure he's the settling down type, Mercy. I think you'd be happier with a man without itchy feet."

Secretly, she knew her pa was right. She wanted a home and a husband and a family, but she never told tell him that. He'd be miserable staying in one place. He'd been like that since her ma had died ten years ago. She loved him too much to mention living in one place.

"We'll see what the future brings. You never know what's around the next corner," she said with a smile. It was one of her pa's sayings. He smiled back but it didn't calm her. She went right back to the entrance and watched the tent next door. Just where was she supposed to meet a man who wanted to put down roots?

"Now Carl is coming up the hill. Quite the welcome from the saloon workers."

"Mercy, Carl's a good guy and an excellent bartender. He

probably thinks since Greg wasn't interested in Shelly he might be interested in a card game or something."

She didn't reply. She went outside instead and the next thing she knew she was in Greg's tent. "Howdy."

Carl tipped his hat to her. "Nice to see you again, Miss Mercy. I was just inviting Greg here to join me for a drink. You're welcome to tag along. I know my customers would love to see you." His words were polite but his tone of voice reminded her of a snake.

"No, thank you anyway. I was just going to go over how to grade the ground, unless you want to show him. There are clouds gathering, and he'll be knee deep in mud and water if it isn't right."

Carl shrugged. "I'll have to defer to your knowledge in these things, Miss Mercy. I know my liquor and my women. Greg, come down and have that drink with me sometime." He tipped his hat again and left.

Greg walked out of the tent and stared up at the sky. "I don't think it's going to rain. Do you have an aversion to spirits?"

"Not in the least. I just didn't want you get taken advantage of by Shelly and Carl."

Greg laughed. "So, you saw Shelly come in, did you?"

"Yes." Mercy waited for more of an explanation but Greg didn't elaborate. Some men were too closed mouthed.

"She stayed for a while," Mercy commented.

"Did she? I hadn't noticed." His lips twitched.

"You're making fun of me, aren't you?" She turned and started out of the tent when she felt Greg's hand on her arm.

"Don't go. I didn't mean to tease you." He waited until she turned toward him. "She just wanted to invite me to the saloon. I turned her down so I guess that's why Carl came up. They want to part me from my money. I'm ill equipped for the goings on at the saloon. I've had whiskey once, I don't play cards, and as for the other…" Red blossomed across his cheeks. "In most ways I'm old enough to be on my own, but I have a lot I haven't experienced. I'll experience it all someday."

"I think you should go home." She gave him a long stare.

"Now why would that be?"

She sighed as she began to climb up to the top of the hill. "You'll change if you stay. You'll become disillusioned and hard. A look of defeat will cross your face more often than not. Right now you're hopeful. I suppose it's not my business, but I don't want you to become like these other men. All they do is chase the gold, drink, and gamble. Did you know most have families somewhere who they promised to send money to but don't? Carl and Shelly are camp followers. They never build a solid structure because they know once a place is panned out, people leave. The towns become empty and another springs up somewhere else."

"You're not hard or defeated," Greg observed, giving her a long assessing look.

"I'm not going to spend all my days mining. I have enough to get me started. I want a plot of land where I can build a small house and have a garden and a few chickens. Perhaps a cow and a horse. I want to live somewhere there is a church and a school. These are things I barely remember from my life before the gold strike."

"Then why don't you go?"

She laughed. "I couldn't leave Pa. But I hold my someday deep in my heart. Even Pa doesn't know. I hold back some of the gold so he can't spend it or gamble it. He doesn't gamble often, but he never wins. I'm looking out for our future." She met and held his gaze. "I hope you won't rummage through our camp looking for my gold."

He reached out and took her hand in his, and she startled.

GREG

"I'd never stand between you and your dreams. You don't have to worry about me."

She gave him a sidelong glance. "Good to know. One neighbor we had peeped at me. I gave him a bloody nose. Pa would have stuck a bullet in him. Like I said, you never know who you'll get as a neighbor. Seems we got lucky with you, even if you are a greenhorn."

He put his hands in his pockets. "A greenhorn at mining but I'm a heck of a cowboy."

She nodded. "I bet that's true. Well, it's time for Pa and me to go to Ima's."

"Go, I'll stand watch."

"You're a fast learner. I'll see you later." She made her way down the hill.

GREG WENT BACK to his tent and grabbed his rifle. Next, he climbed the hill again and sat. The view was good. He could easily see both mines and anyone approaching. The glory and adventure of mining for gold wasn't turning out the way he'd thought. The dangers weren't something he had given much credence to.

People were greedy, he knew that. What was Hugo thinking, allowing his daughter to live in such conditions? Sleeping in a mine. Surrounded by men and loose women. And what about washing? Greg hadn't found a place to bathe yet. What about clean clothes? He'd have to ask Hugo about it. His trousers were so caked with mud, they'd probably stand up themselves. He also needed to send word to Smitty and Lynn and let them know where he was.

He missed them, and he hadn't expected to. He'd been old enough to strike out on his own. They knew what was right and what was wrong, and the lines back home didn't blur as they did out here. He'd have to figure it all out on his own.

The last of the sun had set and it had been a beautiful sight with the pinks and purples. He nodded at Hugo when he spotted them walking back. He put his rifle away and made his way down to the cook tent.

Ima gave him a wide smile. "So you lasted a whole day. Good for you." She handed him a plate, and he loaded it up with pork chops. Ima doled out the potatoes again and he also got some green beans and bread.

He sat down at one of the wooden plank tables and began to eat. Soon enough the table filled up. Many introduced themselves, but he'd never remember their names. The different accents intrigued him. One was from the north, Boston maybe. Another had a Texas drawl. There was a Mexican, and one man had a French accent.

People traveled far to make their fortunes. They asked about his claim, and he answered honestly that he had found nothing, but when he asked about theirs they clammed up. Figured. People were afraid of being shot or claimed jumped.

"Where you from, boy?" The man with the drawl asked.

Being called a boy rankled. "I hale from all over, but most recently Oregon. I traveled the Oregon Trail. And the name is Greg, not boy."

The man grunted. "Sorry, I'm Tex. Nice to meet you. I'm from Texas. Sold my cattle ranch and moved my family here to California."

"Does your family live on your claim?"

"No, I left them about three towns back. My wife was the nagging type, and my daughter was good for nothin'. I left enough money to last a bit, and I've moved from boomtown to boomtown."

Greg stilled. "How long ago was that?" Somehow he dreaded the answer.

GREG

Tex shrugged. "Less than a year I think. She'll have to find someone else, I guess. I really don't care. She never could abide my love of mining."

Greg stood. "Good meeting you." He didn't wait for a reply. His stomach clenched as he handed the plate and cup to Ima. Upon leaving the cook tent, he looked up at the blue sky and gritted his teeth. He wanted to punch Tex in the face. How did someone leave their family behind and forget about them?

Perhaps the same could be said for Hugo. He was just as bad, dragging Mercy around from mine to mine. They called it gold fever for a reason. It made people go out of their minds. It wasn't his problem but he just couldn't understand it. Didn't Tex know what happened to women down on their luck? Heck, his daughter could be working a saloon for all he knew or cared.

Greg had just about walked his anger off when he saw a rustling of his tent flap. Now what? He drew his gun and quickly pulled the flap open. Anger and relief flowed through him.

He holstered his gun. "Shelly what are you doing here? You're not trying to steal my claim are you?" He smiled as though he was teasing, but he was dead serious.

She twisted a lock of blond hair around her finger. "I was looking for you. Carl sent me. You know, one on the house."

"What exactly does that mean?"

"I undress and you have the time of your life."

"Shelly, has anyone ever turned you down?"

She shook her head. "Well, they say no in front of their wives or daughters, but I meet them later. Ask Hugo."

If she thought by telling him Hugo used her it would make her appeal to him, she was wrong.

"Thank you, but I'll pass. Hugo and his daughter are friends of mine, and if Hugo has a claim on you—"

"You think I'm a soiled dove, don't you?"

No matter what he said it would come out sounding the same. "I don't know. You work at the saloon and you just offered…well you offered yourself to me though we really don't know each other. Call it what you want I guess. I'm not in a position to judge another."

Shelly smiled as happy as can be. "Oh, good. I thought you might have disapproved of me. Well, take me up on my offer anytime. Bye, handsome." She sailed out of his tent.

Her perfume filled the small enclosed space, and he took a step outside. There stood Mercy with a big frown on her face.

"What's wrong? Did something happen?" he asked.

"Why would you think something was wrong?" She folded her arms in front her.

"If you could see the way you're looking at me, you'd know what I mean."

Mercy's face turned red, and she dropped her arms to her side. "I saw Shelly go in your tent and it was a very, very long time before she left. Pa wouldn't allow me to go over to your tent while she was there. I can only think of one reason. How much does she make doing the things she does?"

He angled his head. "You have a sharp tongue, Mercy. If you want to know something about Shelly, ask her yourself. I could tell you the rest wasn't any of your business but I don't want you to think badly of me. She was there before I got done with supper. I pulled a gun on her."

"She should know better!" Mercy insisted.

"Yes, she should. She invited me down to the saloon again. I said no. Hard to tell if she was looking around my claim or if the invite was genuine. I think they might want me to play poker and fleece me. I do know how to play. My pa made sure all us boys had a feel for it. He knew how more experienced men take advantage. Plus he didn't want my brother Juan shooting anyone for cheating."

"Your pa sounds like a very smart man. I'd like to meet him someday." She smiled. "I'd best go and brush out my clothes."

"Brush?"

"Yes, until I have a chance to get to one of the watering holes. The stream below is always stirred up with silt. I wear one set of clothes and take them off at night to let them dry. Wear another set the next day and by that evening, the first set has dried mud on it. You can get most of the mud off with a stiff brush. Makes them look halfway decent. Tell you what, I'll show you tomorrow night."

Greg nodded. "Thanks. What about taking a bath around here?"

"It's easy for the men. There is a small pond up yonder. Make sure you bring your own soap and keep an eye on your things on the bank. I usually haul some water and heat it. It's not much but unless I pay to use the bath house, which isn't all that private, it's the best I can do."

"You always look clean to me."

"You're a charmer and a bad liar, Greg Settler, but I'll take it to heart anyway. There aren't many compliments to be had around here."

"Eureka!" Hugo yelled from inside his mine, and Mercy placed her hand over her heart.

"He just put a target on our backs. I need to keep him quiet." She hurried off and ran toward her mine.

Greg followed, looking around. Too many people staring at the Watkins' mine, and most were not wearing looks of happiness. He'd already learned that jealousy over another miner's success could turn deadly with the quickness of a striking snake. He could see the calculated expressions some of the men wore. His rifle was just inside his tent, so he reached in and grabbed it as well as bullets.

Shots rang out just as he stood, and his blood seemed to freeze in his veins.

Hugo staggered out of his mine, a gun in his hand and blood running down his chest, soaking his shirt. He fixed a glazed-eyed stare on Greg. "Mercy," he gasped. "Watch over my Mercy."

Heart racing, Greg went to his friend and knelt beside him. "Where is she?"

"She's been…shot…but…only in the shoulder."

Torn between helping Hugo and going for Mercy, Greg started to stand.

With a sudden burst of energy, Hugo reached out and grabbed Greg's arm. "Please. Take care of her for me." Then he slumped as his breathing became harsh.

Greg nodded and ran into the mine. He nearly tripped over a dead miner, a man he didn't recognize, on his way. Slowly, his eyes adjusted to the dim light. Mercy sat on the ground, her back against the wall of rock, cradling her arm. Greg fell to his knees and gently said her name.

It took a minute but she looked at him. "Pa?"

"He was still alive when I came in to get you, but it doesn't look good."

She simply nodded and allowed him to help her up. She started to run but stopped. "Dizzy."

Greg immediately scooped her up and carried her out. He set her down next to her father.

"Pa? Pa, you old fool. You know better than to let people know you found gold." Tears trailed down her face leaving traces of mud on her cheeks.

With a lot of effort, Hugo pushed his eyes open. "There wasn't…much but…I was relieved to have…found anything. I owe…Carl money." He took a rattling breath. "I love you."

Blood welled at the corners of his mouth, and then he took one final breath.

With her mouth set in a grim line, Mercy closed his eyes and then dried her tears. "Someone get the undertaker!" she called. "Greg, can you help me get him dressed in his good clothes?"

"Of course." He swallowed hard. He was no stranger to hardship and death, but it never got easier. "Come, show me where they are." He scanned the growing crowd. "If you're not here to help, I'd appreciate it if you went on your way." Most wandered off, throwing occasional glances over their shoulders. Smitz, Glad, and Longster stayed.

"We'll dig the grave and help carry the coffin," Smitz said.

"Thank you." Greg helped Mercy up and went into her mine with her.

"Friends of yours?" she asked.

"Your father introduced us. We had a meal together."

"Good enough." She knelt in front of a trunk and pulled out a tattered but clean suit of clothes. "I want him buried in these."

"Now let's get someone to look at your arm," he suggested.

"No, not now."

"Then at least sit for a second so I can put a makeshift bandage on it." He closed the trunk and had Mercy sit on it. He grabbed the cleanest cloth he could fine and dipped it in the warm water near the fire. He gently unbuttoned her shirt and helped her to get her arm out of the sleeve. He sighed in relief. "It looks like it grazed you. I'll bandage it for now but we'll check it later to see if it needs stitching."

She nodded as though she wasn't even listening to him. Her mind was somewhere else. He patched her up and helped her back into her shirt. He then put a coat over her shoulders to hide the wound. This was not the place to show any type of weakness.

"I'll get everything ready, and then we'll walk to the cemetery if that's fine with you." Her pale face and the lost look she wore broke his heart.

He wanted to be angry at Carl, but Hugo had been the one who kept going down to the saloon to gamble. Carl just let him borrow more than he could pay back. That was probably the plan all along. How many other miners had signed their claims over to Carl?

Greg bent and kissed her cheek and then left. Mac promised to stand guard while Greg took care of a few things. Greg had lived a hard life at times but nothing prepared him for the callousness of the men he'd encountered in the mining camp.

The next thing he knew his head felt as though it exploded.

Mercy's heart was as cold as ice. After promising to help her, Greg had left. His things were even gone from his tent. Walking behind the pine coffin to the hole in the ground had been unbearable. She didn't ask where Greg had gone. People lit out all the time, but she'd thought he was different. She'd thought he would at least see her father buried out of respect for the friendship he had been offered.

Shelly of all people stood next to her at the funeral and held her hand. Mercy was grateful and thanked her when it was over. Then Mercy stood alone and watched the men shovel the dirt over the coffin. The coffin her beloved father now lay in. When the last shovelful was thrown on top, she turned and walked up to her claim. It was no surprise to her it had been ransacked.

GREG

Oh, Pa how could you have been so careless? You knew better than to yell in excitement.

Cleaning up would give her something to do. She had no doubt that she'd be visited by buyers and suitors. Who would take over Greg's mine?

Her arm hurt like the dickens, but she pushed it to the back of her mind. She bent and picked up her pa's pipe from the dirt. The smell of the tobacco clutched her heart and refused to let go. She put the pipe in her pocket; it would be something to remember him by.

Drawing herself up, she called out to the man called Glad.

"Yes, ma'am? What can I do for you?"

"I was wondering if I could hire you to guard my mine. You see I have a feeling people are going to think it easy to make me just go away. I can pay you."

"I partner with Mac and Longster on our claim. I'll see if I can be spared. I'll be back."

She rummaged until she found her scale. It had cost her a fortune but it had kept her from being cheated too many times to count. She weighed nuggets until she had enough to more than tempt Glad. Then she buried the scale in one place and hid her gold in another.

"Mercy! Mercy!" She recognized Shelly's voice and hoped against hope it wasn't some type of ruse.

Mercy opened the flap and Shelly ran in breathing hard. "They arrested Greg for killin' your pa. They want to hang him."

Mercy grabbed her hat. "Where? Where are they?"

"The saloon."

Mercy scooped up the gold she'd weighed and started out of the tent. She stopped when she saw Glad and Mac coming toward her. She opened her hand. "Would this be enough to watch the two mines and have one of you come to the saloon to stop a hanging?"

"You got this out of that mine?" Mac asked.

"No, my pa's been gold mining all my life. I always squirreled away some in case."

Glad closed her hand for her. "Take it with you in case you need to buy Greg back. Mac will go with you, and I'll guard the two claims." He shook his head. "Used to be you could trust miners."

With barely a nod of thanks, Mercy ran down to the saloon. She'd heard it called a den of sin before but when she slowed herself to a walk, held her head high, and then entered, she was surprised it was set to look like a jury trial.

"Who accused this man?" she asked loudly as she scanned the tented saloon. She had to quickly glance away from a painting of a naked woman behind the bar. Most of the people there were drunken miners, and Carl seemed to be the man in charge.

Greg looked as though he didn't quite know what was going on. He had blood flowing down the side of his head. She walked toward him but was blocked by one of Carl's men. She heard Mac grunt behind her and motioned for him to stay.

"He's injured. I intend to take a look." She stared at Carl until he gestured for her to move forward.

She sat on a chair next to him and touched his head. He winced and she saw shards of glass in his hair. "Who hit him with a bottle?"

She'd never seen so many men shrug at once before. Standing she put her hands on her hips and glared at Carl. "You are not trying this man."

Carl laughed. "Listen honey, you don't get no say in here."

There was much agreement throughout the saloon.

"So, you're the new sheriff here? You never asked me what happened, and I was there. Makes no sense to me."

"I'll have you put out of here if you don't shut your

mouth. Your pa owed me more than your mine is worth, so I'm taking it. And this greenhorn is going to hang."

She scanned the crowd again and smiled. "I guess you didn't count on the territorial judge being here today, did you?"

Carl's confidence seemed to falter as she frowned and looked around.

A well-dressed man stood and walked over to Mercy. He kissed her on the cheek. "You've grown to be a lovely woman, Mercy. I was so sorry to hear about your pa. I would have been at the burial, but I didn't know it was him that got shot. Now, have a seat and tell me what's going on around here, and for goodness sake someone help this young man. He's getting blood everywhere."

CHAPTER THREE

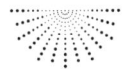

*G*reg was still trying to get his eyes to focus properly when he saw Mercy speaking with a finely dressed gentleman. Next thing he knew, she had a wet cloth against his wound. He closed his eyes for a moment, enjoying the cool sensation.

"What?" he asked as she began picking at his scalp. He still wasn't sure what was taking place.

"Hold on, let me get all the glass out."

"Do you need help, Mercy?" the gentleman asked.

"Greg, this is Territorial Judge Leon Salt. He and my father were good friends."

"Nice to meet you, Judge Salt." Greg winced. Talking made his head pound more. "I just wish I knew what was going on here."

"That, Greg is what I'm going to find out. Don't worry. If Mercy thinks you're a good man, that's all I need to know. But, son, they aim to hang you."

Greg pushed up on the arms of the chair, intending to stand, and was astonished to find that he was tied to it.

"Cut him loose!" Judge Salt demanded.

One of the men who worked for Carl hurried forward and cut Greg loose.

Greg got to his feet, but his legs felt like rubber bands. He stood for a minute and then sat back down, trying to give the appearance of being well.

Carl stepped forward. "It don't matter," he said, talking around a toothpick in his mouth. "The law is the law. Greg Settler shot and killed Hugo Watkins, and he'll hang."

Judge Salt looked amused as he studied Carl from his head to his dusty boots. "Does anyone have a Bible?"

One old bag-of-bones miner came forward carrying a black, leather bound book with raggedy edges and handed it to the judge.

"Carl, is it? Put you hand on the Bible and swear to tell the truth."

Carl's jaw dropped open, but he complied. Next, the Judge told Carl to sit in a chair near Greg."

"Now Carl, think hard. What did you witness of the shooting?"

Carl's face turned bright red. "I saw that man," he made a big deal of pointing at Greg, "He had his rifle and came running out of the mine laughing and practically did a jig right then and there."

The judge walked back and forth in front of Carl as though thinking. He stopped and stared at Carl. "Did he put the rifle down before or after the jig?"

Carl appeared too confused to answer.

"Greg, do you have anything to add?"

"There's a dead miner in the Watkins' mine. I almost tripped over him going in to get Miss Mercy after Hugo stumbled out. No one mentioned him."

Judge Salt nodded. "Where was Mercy?"

"In the mine. She'd been shot. The bullet grazed her arm.

I helped her get outside. Hugo asked me to watch over Mercy."

Carl jumped up. "Convenient, don't you think? The mine is full of gold, and Hugo asks you to watch over Mercy?"

"There is no gold," Mercy said.

"That mine belongs to me!" Carl yelled.

Judge Salt frowned. "Now why would that be?"

"Hugo owed me money for gambling debts."

The judge nodded. "Fine, show me the ledgers where you keep your tallies and maybe we can figure this out."

Carl smirked. "I keep it all in here." He pointed to his head.

"I'm ready to make my ruling," Judge Salt said.

He stood straight and tall as he addressed the people gathered in the saloon. "Greg, what is your last name?"

"Settler, sir," Greg said.

Judge Salt nodded. "Greg Settler is innocent. The dead miner in the Watkins' mine is the killer. Mercy owes nothing to Carl due to lack of evidence. It is no one's business if the mine is a good one or not."

He held up his hand as whispers and protests began. "Quiet." He stared at Mercy for a bit.

"Mercy Watkins, is Greg Settler a good man?"

She blushed. "Yes, Judge he is one of the best men I've ever known."

"Is he in any way abusive toward women?"

Her brow furrowed. "No, he's actually kind."

"Greg, what do you think about Mercy? Is she a shrew? Do you find her unattractive?"

Was he hearing right? He squared his shoulders. "Mercy is a very generous woman, and all you have to do is look at her and see how pretty she is."

Judge Salt smiled widely. "Then there is no reason you shouldn't be married."

Mercy yelped. "I have hired guards to protect me and the mine now."

"Very wise of you, but Mercy, dear, you must agree you need a long-term protection. As of right now I consider you my ward, and I would like for you and Mr. Settler to be married."

Greg's heart sank as Mercy protested. Did she really dislike him so much? He thought they got on fine. Granted, marriage being sprung on him was a bit daunting, but if it meant Mercy would be safe, it was the best way to do it.

"I refuse. Sorry, Salty but I just can't." She ran from the saloon as though Satan himself were chasing her.

The judge helped Greg to stand. "You there!" he yelled to a young miner. "Help this man up to the Watkins mine and leave him there."

Greg shook the judge's hand. "Thank you for everything. If it's any consolation Mercy will be safe with me."

Judge Salt laughed then grew deadly serious. "She'd better be."

As Greg was being helped out of the saloon he heard the judge start lecturing Carl.

MERCY PACED in front of the fire in the living quarters at the front of her mine. The flaps were open, and she was mumbling to herself. Who did these men think they were? They couldn't decide her life!

"Miss Mercy?" Glad asked. "Do we let Settler in, or would you like me to knock him back down the hill?"

She stopped and stared outside. Sure enough Greg was being slowly helped up the hill toward her. "Don't knock him down. In fact, let him in. He may need some stitching. Glad, do you know who the miner was who killed my pa?"

"A lazy good for nothin' looking for a short cut to making it rich. Why he was even up on this part of the camp I have no idea. His mine is almost half a mile from here." Glad frowned. "I do have a theory though."

"What?" she asked impatiently.

"Carl had been spouting off about the debt a few of the miners owed and how it was time to collect one way or the other. In my opinion, the miner was sent to either settle the debt or claim your mine." Glad raked his fingers through his hair. "If you'll have me, miss, I'd like to marry you."

Her hand flew to her throat and she opened her eyes wide. She swallowed hard to give herself a minute. "I so appreciate the gesture, Glad. Judge Salt ordered me to marry Mr. Settler. But I do thank you for looking out for my welfare."

He actually looked relieved. "To tell you the truth I doubt my first wife would have liked you much. You're a bit more independent than she thinks proper."

"I see." She began to pace again. *First wife?* She'd heard a lot of improper things all her life but she was tempted to laugh. It must be hysterics from the events of the day that made her feel that way.

Greg had made it to her claim, and she watched as he thanked some young man. Glad stepped aside and allowed Greg to pass and from the outrageous expression on Greg's face he didn't seem to appreciate her guard.

She held out her hand and led him to her father's bunk. "Let me get a better look at your head." She poured warm water into a basin and grabbed a cloth. She sat almost too close to him. He was the only one she knew who used soap and bothered to clean his teeth. The metal smell of blood was there too.

She gently ran her fingers through his hair to find more shards of glass. After she was satisfied she'd gotten most of them she began to dab at his wound. It was longer than she'd thought but not deep. No stitches would be needed but she wanted to clean the whole cut.

He winced as she dabbed.

"I wish I had some whiskey for you, but the bottle was used on your head."

"I'll be fine. I haven't had much of a chance to talk to you, Mercy. I'm so very sorry about Hugo. He was a man you could be proud to call pa. He might have been filled with wanderlust, but he never left you behind. He loved you so very much, and he was proud of the woman you'd become."

Tears started and the next thing she knew she was sobbing against Greg's shoulder. She tried and tried to rein them in but her heart wouldn't allow her to stop. She went to put her arms around him but stiffened at the pain of her gunshot and it made her cry all the harder. In an instant, her world had changed and she'd been left with one option. No it wasn't an option it was a dictate. She was to marry Greg Settler.

She'd never get her house filled with children or a place to grow roots. Perhaps she'd been destined to move from mine to mine her whole life. Finally, she pulled back, embarrassed. Her vision was blurry, and her eyes stung. They were probably puffy and red. She took a deep breath. She had gold of her own. She could marry and then skip out. San Francisco wasn't so far. She could buy herself a small house and probably live off her money for a while. Slowly she let out her breath.

"I'm sorry I didn't mean to start bawling like a baby." She stood and leaned against a plank of wood at the mine entrance. "I'm glad you weren't hanged but I'm so, so sorry about this wedding thing. It's not what I want at all. But I've always known a woman had no choice. You on the other

GREG

hand, can make a run for it if you like. I can make my own way in life. I'm not your responsibility."

He remained silent.

Turning toward him she studied him. The array of emotions that played across his face amazed her. Relief, worry, anger, much thought, and then resignation. Not what she'd imagined from a prospective groom. Although it hurt, it didn't surprise her. Prospective? Reluctant and forced was the truth of the matter.

"I have a plan," she announced. "We'll pretend we're getting married and just not do it."

Greg's face turned red. "What?"

"Mercy, I thought better of you." She closed her eyes at the judge's voice from behind her.

SHE FIXED a smile on her face and turned. His expression of disapproval stung. "Well, I didn't expect you to come to the mine. It's muddy in here." Shelly stepped from behind the judge. "Shelly, what a surprise."

"How you feeling, Settler?" Judge Salt asked.

"I'll be just fine. Thank you for saving my neck back there."

"I've come to get you two married good and proper. Glad and Shelly will be the witnesses. Greg, can you stand or would you rather you two just sat on the bunk together?"

A grimace flittered across his face. "I wish I could stand that long. A man should stand proudly next to his bride, but I think it best I don't faint in the middle of the ceremony." He held out his hand. "Mercy, come sit with me."

Why did everyone think this marriage such a good idea? Part of her wanted to run and keep running but another part of her wanted a measure of being secure. Greg was the best of the bunch and she did like him. Would they be happy in the long run? Probably not, but options she didn't seem to have.

The seriousness of what was to happen overshadowed the absurdity of it. She could hardly breathe while the words were being said, and she almost choked on the word *obey* in their vows. Call her a liar; she had no plans to obey anyone.

Greg kissed her on the cheek, and before she knew it they were alone. Sighing, she glanced at him. "Well, I guess that's that. Shall I help you to your claim?" She sat frozen in place as she waited for his reply. It wouldn't surprise her if he agreed with her. That was what she wanted wasn't it?

Greg took her hand. "Tell you what. I know this arrangement isn't to your liking, but for better or worse here we are. I'll sleep on your father's bunk for now. But only for now. I have dreams for my life too and they always included a wife and children." He sounded dead tired. "Now take off your shirt."

Her eyes widened, and her heart pounded. "I most certainly will not." She lifted her chin ready to battle it out.

"I want to tend to your arm."

"It's fine," she clipped.

"Mercy, I want to be sure it's cleaned out properly. Please?"

With a sigh of defeat, she stood and poured warm water in a bowl. Then she gathered a clean cloth and a clean bandanna that could be used to bandage it. "No stitches."

"I can't promise until I see it."

She couldn't help but frown at him as she put the items down and unbuttoned her shirt. Turning away from him, she took her arm out of the sleeve and then clasped the rest of the shirt to cover herself. She then sat down next to him. He was so gentle, the gentlest man she'd known. He cleaned out the wound, and she sat still.

"It must hurt," he murmured.

She nodded. "It does but I've had worse. It doesn't need stitching, does it?"

"No, it stopped bleeding. I'm going to wrap it for you, though. You're very brave. Heck, my sisters would have been wailing loud enough for people to hear for miles."

Mercy shrugged her shoulder. "Like I said, I've had worse injuries and nothing to dull the pain." She smiled. "Maybe we should have had some whiskey while we were in the saloon."

His lips thinned, and anger flashed in his eyes. "You do know it's not over with Carl, even though your judge friend told him to forget it. We need to be on guard. He'll think us weak now with our wounds."

"Good thing I hired Glad and Mac then, isn't it?"

"How much did you have to pay them?"

"More than enough. I've saved gold nuggets all my life. I can get by if I need to."

"I wouldn't expect anything else." A smile tweaked his lips. "You're very independent."

"That's why this marriage isn't going to work out. I have no intention of obeying you. I thought you should know up front so we know where we stand with each other."

"Well that's fine. I don't intend to obey you either. I need to talk to Glad or Mac and then I'll need to sleep." He stood, went outside and returned with a bag full of his things. He put his own blanket and pillow on the bunk. "I'd kiss you goodnight but I'm as weak as a baby calf."

"I understand." She watched as he rolled into the bunk, clothes and all. Yawning, she did the same.

CHAPTER FOUR

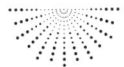

*G*reg was in agony. If Mercy brushed her body against his one more time he was going to explode. It was tight quarters in the mine shaft, and he tried to explain it to her, but she told him she knew more than he did about mining and this was how it was done. She seemed to enjoy the contact with him. Her eyes seemed to glow every time she did it.

If he hadn't known she was innocent, he'd have thought she was doing it on purpose. "We need to widen the whole mine."

Her brow furrowed. "What are you taking about? If you find gold we dig that way. It's a waste of time and energy to do any more digging." She tilted her head. "You're afraid down there, aren't you? Lots of people don't realize it until they have to spend a lot of time underground. Tell you what. You gather all the rocks and bring them up here to examine them. I'll do the hard part."

He shook his head. "Why do you always think the worst of me?"

"There's no shame in being afraid."

"Shoot me now," he mumbled.

"What was that?"

He shook his head. "Nothing. Let's get back to work."

Mercy stared at him, shrugged her shoulders, and swung the pickaxe. She was better than most men with that thing. There was not one wasted movement, and she hit the rock hard.

She stopped and scowled. "Now what?"

He grinned. "I was just thinking you could probably win if we arm wrestled."

"Don't think, just know. Of course I'd win." She went back to work.

A bit later, there was a straining noise, and they both stopped and stared at each other.

"What is that?" Greg asked. His stomach clenched.

"We get out now, go get timber and shore it up."

Some heavy rocks began to fall from above them and they hightailed it out of there.

It took Greg a moment to catch his breath. "It's dangerous down there."

"It's not a job for the faint of heart. I'm beginning to think mining isn't for you."

He sat down on his bunk. "I'm thinking it's too dangerous for a woman. I don't think you should go into the shaft anymore."

Her jaw dropped and she crossed her arms in front of her. "You don't tell me what to do," she said with an edge to her voice.

"I am your husband."

Mercy glared at him and stomped outside. He quickly followed.

"Where are you going?" he asked.

"I'm going to get the lumber. You're welcome to help if

you like. Or you can sit on the bunk and decide if you're going mine your own mine without me."

She started down the hill. "Glad can you keep an eye on our mines?"

"I'd be happy to," Glad said.

"For heaven's sake!" He hurried after her. "This is a good opportunity for you to show me what kind of wood we use. I'm sure there are different sizes and types."

"You get what you get," she said without looking at him.

"Why is that?

"The better timber is saved for buildings and houses. Once in a while, you get lucky and you find some at an abandoned mine. But this place is becoming so full, we'll have to buy some. I have a hammer and nails. A strong back is also required." Mercy continued to walk without so much as a glance at him.

He'd certainly ruffled her feathers. He shouldn't have told her mining was too dangerous for a woman. She knew so much more than he. He was probably the dangerous one. He could make a mistake and bring the whole ceiling down on them.

"Mercy?"

"What is it?" She still didn't look at him.

"I apologize for my outburst. You have more experience than me, and I shouldn't have said it was too dangerous for you. Where I'm from, men protect their women."

She snorted. "Woman can do just fine. They just need to know how to shoot. Fear of shooting can be a problem for some women, but I'd rather shoot first and ask questions later."

He nodded. He'd best remember that.

She stopped in front of three piles of wood. "Now let me show you. This here wood, is fine wood. See how nice and straight it is? That's for building. Now you can pick from the second or third pile depending."

"Depending on what?"

"How long you want to live." She smiled at an approaching man. He was nicely dressed and there wasn't a splat of mud on him. "Jamie, nice to see you." Her voice was as sweet as sugar.

Jamie smiled back, took her hand and kissed the back of it. "The very sight of you has brightened my day, Miss Mercy." He still held her hand. "Sorry I was to hear about your dear father. If you need anything, I can buy the mine from you if you need me to."

Mercy withdrew her hand from him. "Jamie, this is Greg. He's my husband. We're going to stick it out for a while. In fact, we need some timber."

"Hearty congratulations on your nuptials. It's nice to meet you, Greg." He stuck out his hand.

Greg shook Jamie's hand. Just as he expected, the other man's hands were as soft as a baby's bottom. If Greg hadn't already been put off by Jamie's over the top conversation, he'd dislike him from his handshake alone.

"You must be new around here."

Greg nodded. "Yes, I'm new and as soon as I laid eyes on Mercy, well I couldn't allow her to get away, now could I?" He felt the heat of Mercy's stare. "We need some wood."

Mercy was quick in picking what she wanted, and Jamie promised to have it delivered to her claim. Greg took Mercy's hand as they walked away. They hadn't gone far before she pulled her hand away.

"Couldn't allow me to get away? Gah!"

"He was staring at you like you were a piece of candy."

She stopped walking. "He was? Well, I didn't notice. Men stare all the time because I'm one of the only single females around who doesn't work for Carl. I've had nearly fifteen marriage proposals."

"That's a lot." He rubbed the back of his neck. "No one tickled your fancy?"

"I don't have time for miners. I've seen too many and they don't interest me in the least."

"What type of man does interest you?"

"I suppose you, since we're married. I might as well get to know you. Then if I decide I don't like you, we don't need to talk to each other."

"A marriage of not talking? That wouldn't be a happy one." He continued on back to the mine, not caring if he was walking too fast for her. With his long stride he easily outpaced her. What if he decided he didn't like her? Had she thought of that? Maybe it was time to leave mining behind. He came, he'd given it a try. Now he was ready to train horses. Funny how he just had to get away to prove himself, and what he wanted most was to be back near his family. He wanted his own spread of course.

"Wait! You walk too darn fast."

He turned and waited, watching as she hurried up the hill. She was a pretty woman, but would he have chosen her if he'd had a choice? He took off his hat and ran his fingers through his hair. It really didn't matter. It was done.

She stopped and stared at him. "I guess I was a bit hasty in my statement. It'll take some time to get to know each other. I'm looking forward to it. I guess I just don't like being cornered and told what to do. Everyone always has the upper hand, and I'm tired of it."

"I can understand that," he said softly before he took her hand and held it the rest of the way to the mine. "It's going to be hot today."

"If it's too hot we can sleep during the day and work at night. We use the oil lamps to see anyway, so it really doesn't make a difference. Some miners work in shifts. That might work better for you, so I'm not always in your way."

He opened the flap and they walked inside. "Mercy, if we do that we won't get to know each other. Plus I don't feel comfortable thinking you'd be up here sleeping alone. What if someone comes to attack again?"

She reached under her bunk and drew out a gun belt. "Fine, we'll do it your way. I'll wear this from now on. Plus you need someone to teach you the ropes."

He looked down at the ground trying to think of a way to bring up leaving. He looked at her. Would she be comfortable living in a house? "Mercy, you once mentioned wanting to have a home with children. Did you mean that?"

Confusion played across her face. "Someday, yes. Right now I'm going to start digging toward your mine and see if there is gold there while we wait for the timber."

Before he could get a word out, a gunshot exploded through the air, making his ears ring. Mercy bent and then stood up, holding the biggest rattler he'd ever seen.

She shook her head. "Now, where do you suppose this came from?"

"It could have crawled in."

"Somehow, I doubt it." She took off at a fast pace with the rattler dangling from her hands. Greg struggled to follow her as she marched right into the saloon, but he arrived just as she threw the snake on the ground.

Carl walked from behind the bar and stared at the rattler. "You don't see many of those around here."

She widened her stance and put her hand on her gun. "Exactly what I was thinking. So, who do you suppose put it in my mine?" Her eyes narrowed as she stared at Carl.

Greg's stomach dropped. He put his arm around her waist and turned her toward the door.

Mercy shrugged his arm away. "Let go of me. I know it

was Carl who put it there. He's wanted my mine from the very beginning!"

An angry murmur surged through the saloon, making Greg nervous. Carl had a lot of friends, and those who weren't friends owed him in some way. Mercy was sure to get herself shot and Greg wasn't about to let that happen.

"Mercy, let's go home."

She shook her head. "It's about time someone stood up to him and that someone is going to be me. We can't go around living in fear that Carl is going to try to jump our claims. He's done it before in other towns. I want him stopped!"

"Listen, Mercy, think what you want, but I had nothing to do with that stinkin' snake. Lots of people jump claims. If you want to make this a gunfight, well darlin' your husband better get a coffin built." Carl's voice was steady, but he was ready to shoot Mercy if it came to it, of that Greg had no doubt.

"Mercy, we're going to need more proof," Greg said. "He's going to shoot you, and you'll never have your revenge."

She finally turned her head and looked at him. She looked angry and distraught. His heart went out to her, but he resolved to stay firm for her sake and his. "Let's go see if the timber has been delivered yet. We have mining to do."

Taking a deep breath, she nodded. "Let's go. Nothing is getting accomplished here."

Carl smiled. "Don't forget to take your snake."

Greg wanted to haul off and punch Carl, but he had to get Mercy home. "Keep it." He had plenty of insults he could have said, but that would only have made things worse.

They walked out of the tent and Mercy looked as though she was waiting to be yelled at. He didn't say a word. He just walked up to the claim. "The wood is here. You might as well show me what to do."

Mercy's eyes widened, but she quickly looked the wood

over and grabbed a few pieces. "Come on, let me show you how to shore up the mine."

He took the wood from her and followed her into the mine. Her hips swayed as she walked, and he enjoyed how her pants showed the outline of her figure. A smile pulled at his lips. What would she say if he told her not to wear pants anymore? He suppressed a chuckle; he wasn't feeling lucky enough to win that fight.

They stopped midway along the shaft they'd been working in, and she showed him how to brace the mine. "We'll be doing this more and more as we dig."

"I'm impressed with your knowledge, Mercy. I shouldn't be though seeing as how you've been mining for years but I look at you and see how beautiful you are and I don't know. I guess I expect you to know more about dressmaking and recipes than mining."

It seemed interminable until she tilted her head and gazed at him. He'd said something wrong, dang it.

"I'll take that as a compliment. I'm not empty headed with nothing but recipes stored in my brain. I can cook but I can do a lot of things. Now I'll start here, and why don't you go in the direction of your mine? Maybe you were lucky after all picking a spot."

It was hard work lifting the pickaxe time after time and Mercy was faster at it then he was. Bending down, he picked up a large rock to examine it, ready to toss it aside when he saw gold.

"Mercy, I found—"

Before he could finish speaking, she had her lips on his. She pressed so hard it was uncomfortable. He drew his head back a bit and then he moved his mouth over hers. Her lips were sweet and supple against his. She moved with him for a second then she punched him in the arm.

"What?"

GREG

"Are all men alike? Look, first of all you never say what you found. People are always listening, and I'm not burying another so soon. Second, don't kiss me like you enjoy it. I'm not really sure you even like me. And third... Well I'm sure there is a third, but I want to see that rock first."

She took it and brought it closer to the lamp. Her eyes widened and she sat down hard staring at it. "Too bad Pa is gone. Or maybe it's just as well. He'd probably have given the mine to Carl for his debts sooner or later." A lone tear spilled down her face. She hastily wiped it away. "Come here. I won't hit you again."

He sat down next to her, and though his instinct was to put his arm around her, he didn't think it would be appreciated. "So?" he whispered.

"This whole hunk is it. No one can know about it. We will just call it...*it*. We, my friend, are in the most danger of our lives, and it's up to us to keep ourselves safe. We can't get Glad or Mac to stand guard again. We can't disrupt our routine. And for heaven's sake, don't go spending any of the money."

It was serious business, but she made it sound downright scary. He nodded. "I'll do what it takes to protect you. And Mercy? I do like you." He stood and held his hand out to help her up.

SHE HID the lump of gold at the bottom of a pail and put regular rocks on top of it. She handed it to Greg and had him carry it out of the mine to their living quarters in the front. He cocked his brow at her. "One small step at a time. While I fish it out of the pail why don't you yell at me for confronting Carl about the snake? Make it loud."

Hiding her smile behind her hand she watched him furrow his brow.

"Well? What's wrong?" she asked.

"I'm not sure what to say. I don't want you getting mad."

"Just say the snake could have just crawled in there or something."

He nodded. "How do you know that snake was put there by Carl?"

"Louder," she whispered as she took the rocks out.

"It could have crawled into the mine. That's what snakes do, and throwing down at Carl was not a bright thing to do. What if he took offense? What if he decided to shoot you and then me?"

"Stop yelling at me!" She winked as she examined the gold.

"We just got married. I don't want to be a widower before I've had my wedding night!"

She jerked her head up and she dropped her jaw. "That is no one's business, Greg Settler!!"

He smiled and nodded. "A man has his rights, you know!"

"Halleluiah!" Someone from outside shouted.

"Stop it," she hissed.

Greg frowned at her and shrugged. "What's wrong?"

"The fight idea was a bad one, so let's just stop." Her face heated. How could he yell about something so personal to the whole camp? They all knew now she hadn't done whatever it is that wives do.

He studied her until she told him to stop looking at her. Then he sat next to her on her bunk.

"I'm sorry. I wasn't thinking about how it sounded to others. Mercy, I'd never purposely embarrass you. I don't think more than a handful of miners heard you."

"Are you loco? People always thought I was a bit off for being a woman working the mines but now…" Her shoulders slumped. "It's not your fault. I'm just not wife material. I don't know how to act like a woman. I'm a great miner, and I was a wonderful daughter, but I'm not anything else."

Greg reached out and caressed her cheek. "Some things just don't come naturally. I'm not sure who'd you learn from out here. I like you just the way you are. You don't try to hide who you are. Heck, if I was a girl out here I'd have disguised myself as a boy."

She nodded and gave him a brief smile. "My dad wanted me to, but I refused. I can't be something I'm not."

"See that's what I'm talking about. You are true to yourself. Don't worry about those yahoo's out there. They have no couth. Outside the mine, we'll hold hands and smile at each other. That should dispel any rumors I started. So? What about it?"

"It is huge. I'd like to go back to the mine, but first I need a place to hide this." She lifted the empty chamber pot and dug a hole, put the gold in it and covered it back up with the pot. "Look away."

"Why?"

"I'm going to make use of the chamber pot, and then probably no one will move it."

He nodded and turned his back.

"How did you and Hugo work out meals and such? I know you went together while I guarded, but what did you do before that? Did you go to the cook tent alone?"

He heard her finish up and then the rustling of clothes.

"You can turn back around. Ima always fixed a plate for me. You just bring the extra tin plate and all is good. She's good people."

"Yes she is."

Sighing, Mercy opened the flaps and allowed people to catch a glimpse of them. "We need to act like we're happy."

"Easy enough," Greg whispered as he stood behind her

and wrapped his arms around her. He then kissed her neck while she laughed.

"We just have to show our affection for each other," he said.

"I didn't know you felt anything for me," she whispered as she smiled.

Greg turned her in his arms and gazed into her eyes. "I like you, and that is much more than many marriages start with. I admire you, your courage, your knowledge; I like your cheerfulness and your stubbornness. Plus, you are a very attractive woman."

"I'm stubborn?"

Greg laughed and pulled her close. Close enough he could feel the heat of her body without actually touching. "I give you all kinds of compliments, and the only thing you remember is the stubborn part?"

Feeling unbalanced wasn't something she was used to. "I heard you, but I thought it was for show."

"No one can hear me now." He gave her a big grin that set her stomach to feeling as though butterflies were flying around in it.

"I like you too."

He still grinned. "That's all? I'm not brave or a manly man? How about handsome as sin?" He laughed and people began to stare. Leaning in he kissed her cheek. "I'll work on it."

"Work on what?" She felt as though she was on fire.

"The way you see me. You'll find me irresistible eventually."

This time she laughed loud and clear. He was right. People would forget she hadn't done her duty soon enough. She liked him. A shiver rippled through her. He seemed to really like her too. She frowned. Was he pretending?

"Hey, what's the frown for?"

GREG

"Greg is this all for show? Or…"

"I think we'll get on just fine, and we'll have a good marriage. I'm going to the cook tent and I'll bring food back. Keep your sidearm near you."

She nodded, feeling warm all over. She sat back down on her bunk and watched her husband. He certainly was fine of form. His shoulders were nice and wide and his legs looked to be well muscled. He washed daily and there was an air of confidence about him that she liked.

Leaning back against the wooden wall, she smiled. She'd just had her first kiss. Did it count if it was meant to keep someone's mouth shut? Taking a deep breath, she sighed happily. The kiss certainly ended much better than it had started. Warmth spread through her. He'd moved his mouth over hers until she'd liked it and wanted more. There was more to this marriage thing than doing women's work. Perhaps he would kiss her again soon.

Movement in the distance drew her attention. Shelly was walking toward her, and she groaned.

"Howdy," Shelly said with a great big smile that wasn't reflected in her eyes.

"Hey, Shelly. Who—I mean what brings you here?"

"I was just stretching my legs a bit. I see you and your scrumptious husband are getting along. I guess I won't have the pleasure of seeing him again."

Mercy shrugged. "He's around. I'm sure you'll see him."

"I meant, well you know. He's quite the eager one in bed. You two are probably very comfortable sharing a bunk. You're lucky, you know."

Shelly wanted to get her mad. "He is, we're comfortable, and yes I'm very lucky. I'd hate to ask you to leave but he should be here soon and I'd like to spend time with him outside of the mine."

Shelly didn't seem to know what to do next. She certainly

wasn't well practiced in being catty. "Just tell him I stopped by."

"I certainly will. Thanks for visiting!"

Shelly's eyes widened. "Yes, well good bye." She turned and hurried away.

That darn Carl probably sent her up here to cause trouble. That could easily have been her own fate. Women didn't have many choices especially in the boomtowns. But Shelly acted comfortable in her revealing clothes. Mercy shook her head. She'd feel ashamed prancing around that way. Then again she didn't have Shelly's tiny figure. Greg probably didn't know how Mercy looked. She always wore an oversized shirt over her pants to hide what she could. Tiny, she wasn't.

CHAPTER FIVE

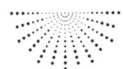

Later that night, Greg brought Mercy down into the mine to see where he'd found the gold. She held the lamp up high and her intake of breath was loud. She turned toward him with wide eyes. "Oh, my."

She looked again, and this time she touched it and tapped here and there with a small pick. "We have work to do."

"We need to get it out quickly," he said, feeling an urgency take over.

"No. We need to cover it with wood. It'll take a long while to get all that gold out. I'm both excited and sick to my stomach," she whispered. "We're rich as can be, and we're in danger. We'll need to take precautions and rig up signals so we know if someone is coming. Come on."

Greg followed her out of the mine. She grabbed his hand and pulled him down onto one of the bunks with her. Her eyes were bright as she smiled at him.

"We'll need to work out a few hand signals and we'll need to whisper without appearing to whisper," she said.

"I can always hug you to whisper in your ear. No one will find that strange."

She nodded. "I like that idea. We'll need to string cans together and put them at the entrance to the tunnel. Anyone coming will hit them with their leg and the noise will alert us. We'll also need a way to move the gold out of here when we leave without anyone knowing we have it."

"We do?" There was so much he didn't know. He'd heard the stories of gold on the ground for the taking. Not that he believed that, but he hadn't thought it would be such hard work. They had actually found something but it looked as though there were many poor miners out there.

"We can't be obvious when we load up. People will be watching and if our load looks heavy, they'll know we have a big strike here. We need them to think we're leaving because we struck out."

His jaw dropped. Mercy was practically giddy at the prospect of lying. Excitement coursed through him. Was there really that much gold on their claim? He understood her giddiness.

"Fine, first show me how to make an alarm from cans, then we'll figure out how to move the gold," he said as he took the lamp from her. He reached out and took her hand. "I think we can act happy. People will think we're in love."

THE LOOK she gave him was a wistful one. He wasn't sure how much acting either of them would have to do. She was growing on him with every touch and every glance. He had the feeling if she didn't want him around, he wouldn't be. She could be as stubborn as all get out and he'd know not to touch her.

Not that they were ready to consummate the marriage, but he felt comfortable enough she wouldn't be barring him from the mine. He led them up back up to their living quarters. She pulled her hand away and grabbed a crate of cans and a roll of twine.

"Are you sure you never did this before? I though all boys put these in front of their forts to keep girls out."

"My childhood was a bit different."

"You didn't grow up in a house with two parents?"

"I'm pretty sure I did until I was five. Then my parents were killed, and I had to run with only the clothes on my back." He closed his eyes and he could still see the bright red blood gushing from the gunshots both parent had. Someone had wanted their land was what he'd been told later.

"I hid in the woods all night and then somehow made it to my uncle's farm. My aunt promised me a place to live but my uncle hated my father for some reason and refused to have me under his roof." He sighed and gave her a sad smile.

"I was then sent to the local orphanage, which was really full. Lots of hardship I suppose is why there were so many kids there. I did get adopted by some folks who seemed really nice, and I was ever so grateful. But when I got to their farm, I was one of ten boys and there really wasn't enough food to go around. I was a scrawny kid and wasn't up to fighting the older boys. One day a wagon pulled up with the sheriff riding next to it, and they took me back to the orphanage. I was ten or eleven by this time. The orphanage didn't seem so bad comparatively."

"How'd you get this far west?" she asked.

"I was finally adopted along with four other boys by a real good couple, John and Lynn Downey. They were great people, and they didn't want me for labor. They wanted me for me. We all worked side by side for a few years, and then one day they sat us down and asked how'd we like to go to Oregon." Greg rubbed his neck. The memories were bittersweet. "John died not too far into the trip, and then our brother Danny died too. I wasn't sure our ma would be able to go on. She cried and cried. Smitty, he's our pa now, and took good care of her and us, and we made it with two more brothers we found at a fort. Then Freddie and Aaron died. It was a bad time. I also have two sisters. Oh, and I have a three-year-old brother named Brian. Not long before I left, two new kids came. One we think was three or four named Oscar and a baby named Alex. Then Ma had a baby girl named Rose."

"Wow, you've had what my pa would have called a colorful life. I'm surprised you left, but itchy feet are hard to keep still." Mercy picked up a can and a knife. She poked a whole near the top of the can for the twine to fit through.

"I think I wanted to prove to myself I was capable. I plan to go back someday." He picked up a can and fished his knife out. He then copied Mercy's actions.

"Does someday mean in ten to twenty years?"

"No, I'm missing them already."

She stiffened and turned her head away. "So, you'll be leaving soon?"

"In a few weeks, I would think. How long would it take to get…it?"

"Not knowing how far back into the rock it goes, I'm not sure." She continued to get the cans ready. She then threaded the cans through and made two long lines.

A frown pinched Greg's brow. Maybe she didn't want to leave the mines. He'd thought she'd be happy about it, but she was awfully quiet. Too bad he didn't know her better. The silence wasn't a comfortable one, and he wasn't sure what to say.

"Once we have these strung, where do we put them?" he asked.

"One will go right inside the mine, low to the ground. The other I was thinking would be attached to one of the flaps. If someone tries to enter we'll hear it."

"They could just use the other flap."

She nodded and smiled. "I've been thinking on it, and if we move the fire pit to the right just a bit, people will natural come in through the left side."

"You know, for a girl, you're awfully smart." He grinned as she frowned.

"I'm sure you meant to say something else didn't you?" She cocked her brow.

"I certainly did," he laughed. "I meant to say my beautiful wife is very intelligent."

"That's better. Now we have to be real quiet hanging these cans then we can open the flap and hold hands or something."

The *or something* sounded good to him. They worked slowly together and finally got their alarm system in place. Then he opened the left flap. They sat together on his bunk but Mercy was as stiff as a pair of pants that hadn't been washed in a month.

"I know something is wrong but I don't know what. Talk to me Mercy. Was it something I did?" He took her hand in his and stroked the back of it with his thumb.

"It's nothing really. I'll just miss you when you go is all. But don't you worry I'll be just fine. I can take care of myself, you know. No one will get the jump on me."

Greg let go of her hand and leaped up. "You're not coming with me? I thought maybe you were beginning to like me. I'm as stupid as a jack—" He walked out of their mine and went into his tent. Women were complicated. He'd heard his pa say so often, but Mercy was downright impossible to figure out.

He paced back and forth. Didn't she say her father was the one who wanted to mine, not her? He could have sworn that she wanted a house and family. How could he have gotten that wrong? Or maybe she had said it but changed her mind. He'd been a fool thinking they could have a good life together.

His anger turned to hurt. He'd begun to fall in love with his wife. He shouldn't have allowed that to happen. She fascinated him, and he'd begun to long for her. He was a sucker. Back home he almost married a pregnant girl to keep her from becoming an outcast. It wasn't his child, and he'd hardly known the girl. He'd dodged that bullet.

Here he was again but this time he was tied by marriage vows. He could stay with her and mine but wouldn't that just make him a fool? He could leave her, but he'd worry about her every day. Maybe he could work extra slow so he'd have more time to convince her to come with him. But did he really want someone who didn't want him?

Mercy lay on her bunk thinking almost all night. Greg hadn't come back, and her stomach was in knots and her heart ached. It was understandable why he'd want to leave her behind. She lacked social graces, she walked and talked like a man, and she was no great beauty. She wouldn't know the first thing to say to his mother or sisters. They probably drank tea out of china cups and she was used to tin. Heck, she didn't even drink tea.

She didn't own any of the undergarments other women did. All she had was a black faded dress that was too short for her and a bit tight across the chest. Her hair had mud caked in it more times than not. Sadness filled her. No, she wasn't the wife for Greg. He was destined for better things. He could just leave and not tell anyone he had married. They'd never consummated the marriage, so he really was free to go.

The cans made an awful racket, and she rolled onto the ground, gun in hand. She just missed being shot. Her heart

GREG

was pumping as she took aim and shot. Hearing a yelp didn't bring her any pleasure. The killer was still alive. She rolled to the other side of the living quarters and then slowly got up and ran into the mine, jumping over the cans strung just inside the entrance. She ran until she was behind some of the wood that shored up the mine. Her whole body shook as she waited. The killer would probably be on the lookout for more cans.

Her back hurt as she pressed harder against the jagged rock. She took a deep breath and let it out again trying to calm herself. It didn't work. How was she going to shoot with her hands shaking? There was so much riding on her killing the man. Finally she got herself together and aimed the gun at the entrance. She planned to take him down with one shot.

She was so focused on killing she didn't hear Greg calling her at first. Thank God, she finally heard him before she shot him. Slowly, she lowered her gun and slumped against the stone wall. Her body shook in earnest now, and she didn't try to stop it. Tears pricked at her eyes. What was going to happen to her when Greg left in a few weeks?

His stride was purposeful as he walked toward her and he pulled her into his arms, holding her tight. "I thought I lost you."

She could feel him shaking too. "Where is he?"

"Dead. Your aim was good. You hit his chest and it took a few minutes for him to die." He pulled away and looked her over then pulled her into his arms again. "I should have been here. I'm so sorry."

She wrapped her arms around his waist and held on with everything she had. She wanted to stay in the safeness of his arms always. Maybe if she showed her usefulness, he'd take her with him when he left. But how?

"Let's get you out of here. I bet a cup of coffee sounds

good about now." He let go of her, took the gun from her and held her hand. "Did the cans alert you?"

"Yes, I wasn't asleep but they gave me time to roll off my bunk. I can't believe I'm still alive."

He led her to his bunk and sat her down. The flap was still open and a crowd had gathered outside. Greg poured her a cup of the mud like coffee they usually had warming near the fire. He handed to her and sat next to her.

"Why don't you close the flap?" Mercy asked.

"Maybe this guy didn't know we're married and thought we'd made a strike. I want everyone to see we're together and happy."

"Are we?"

He frowned. "Are we what?"

He was so clueless she didn't want to answer. She shrugged her shoulders. "I don't know. *Are* we happy, or should I pretend?"

He took the cup from her and set it on the ground. He took both of her hands in his and looked into her eyes. "I'm not pretending. I'm happy you're my wife. Pretend if you have to."

She shook her head. "I don't need to pretend. I'm happy as long as I'm with you." She hoped they'd be together much longer than she thought.

"We'd best go outside and answer any questions," he said.

Pulling away she stated into his eyes. "What type of questions?"

He touched her cheek. "Honey, you just shot someone. There are bound to be questions. Just be honest as much as you can." He stood and took her hand, pulling her up beside her.

Her body felt chilled without his against her. "I'm not sure. I killed a man, Greg. This is a bad idea."

"You have to show you did nothing wrong. Nothing that anyone of them wouldn't have done to protect themselves."

Biting her lip she glanced down at the dirt. She could do this couldn't she? She gave him a slight nod and followed his lead out the mine. Of course Carl was one of the men in the front. His mocking grin nearly had her running back to safety.

Greg stood straight and tall, while he squared his shoulders. "We appreciate all of you coming to make sure we're fine. Truth is, we're shook up. There's been too many shootings in the name of greed. Has any of you seen gold from this mine?"

The miners looked from one to another and shook their heads.

"Frankly, Mercy and I have been busy with other things than mining at the moment. I can only conclude it was your doing, Carl." Greg cocked his brow as he stared at Carl.

Carl spit on the ground and then he frowned. "Not this time." He smiled mockingly.

"Perhaps I'm being a bit hasty in my judgement," Greg conceded. "Does anyone know who this dead man is?"

Until that moment Mercy had avoided looking at the dead body. She glanced, and her stomach churned. His brown eyes were still open and his shirt was blood soaked. She'd always been so proud to be good with a gun, her aim was true, but killing was different. "It's Wesley," she muttered.

Greg turned toward her. "Wesley who?"

"He's traveled from strike to strike, same as me and Pa. We were on friendly terms at one time, but he tried to, well he cornered me and tried. Anyway, Pa told him to never darken our door again. He was to pretend he didn't know us because we would never claim him for a friend again. Wesley was livid but he was also lucky my pa didn't take his head off.

I was afraid to leave our tent for weeks after that." Her throat tightened as she remembered that awful day.

Greg put his arm around her waist and pulled her close. "This is my fault. We had a small argument and I stormed into my tent leaving her alone. I should have been the one to protect my wife from evil."

A few of the miners looked surprised. Greg had been right, there were those who didn't know they were married. Mercy laid her head on his shoulder. She couldn't stop herself from staring at dead Wesley.

"Who's going to pay to have Wesley buried?" Carl asked, still smirking.

Glad pushed his way to the front. "I'll do it for free. Miss Mercy has been through enough. I'll remove the body now."

Mercy nodded and tried to find a smile within her but there wasn't one.

"We appreciate that, Glad," Greg said. "Any other questions before we go to bed?"

There were a few whistles and cat calls, but it was brief. Mercy held her breath, waiting.

Carl stepped even closer. "So let me get this straight. A man who tried to attack you before ends up dead by your own gun? I find that to be highly suspicious. You harbored a grudge against poor old…old…" He turned to one of his men who whispered *Wesley*. "Wesley. He was walking by and you shot him."

She shook her head. "That's not how it happened. Not at all. I was in my bunk worrying about the fight I'd had with my husband. Someone pushed open the flap and rattled the cans I had strung. I rolled out of bed and there was a shot from outside. I shot back. I didn't know the shot was deadly. He yelped, and I figured I got his shoulder or something."

"Enough questions," Greg announced loudly. "There was no revenge. Wesley shot first. Mercy and I put up the cans so we'd know if anyone was walking in on us while we were… well before we had our fight…"

Mac laughed. "No explanation needed. The events sound true enough to me. I didn't like that weasel Wesley no how. Come on, fellas, let's give the newlyweds some privacy." He turned and most of the men followed all but Carl.

Mercy needed to get away from Carl. She let go of Greg and went back inside their living quarters and sat on the bunk behind the closed flap. She'd had enough for one day, one week, one month. Carl had been angling to have her blamed for a wrongful death. Why wouldn't that man leave her be? Maybe it was time to leave while both she and Greg were still alive.

She wrapped her arms around her middle as fear filled her. If Carl kept pushing, she might be hanged. Many of the miners owed him money and they'd do as he asked. She rocked back and forth but she couldn't comfort herself. She'd seen plenty of violence living among men but she had killed a man. Even though he was a piece of scum, he had been a person. She was going to hell, she just knew it.

Greg finally came in, and he put more wood on the fire. Then he sat next to her and gathered her in his strong arms. Finally she felt safe enough to cry. Once she started she couldn't seem to stop.

She cried for her father, taken from her too soon. She cried for the young girl Wesley had tried to attack, she cried for the life she took, and she cried because she knew someone like Greg could never really truly love a person like her. He cared so much about his family, but he'd be too embarrassed to bring her home. Her torment lessened as Greg stroked her back. She stopped sobbing and was surprised how quiet it was. All she could hear was the pounding of Greg's heart along with the hissing and spitting of the fire.

"As soon as we get the g—*it*, I'd like you to drop me at a nice town. I can buy a dress along the way and find some way to get all this mud from my body. I bet there are all kinds of things a woman with money can do. I could open a business, or find a rich husband."

Greg stiffened. "No."

"I want to be someone else, and you'd be rid of me."

"No."

She pulled out of his embrace and studied his face. "You've been kinder to me than anyone other than my pa. The only thing of worth I can give to you is your freedom. And your mind will be at ease. I'll be somewhere safe and not your problem." She tried to give him a tender smile but from his stormy expression she must have failed.

"You are not a problem. You are my wife, and we will be together. If you want to leave we will leave together. I don't want my freedom. I want us to have a happy life, together. A good life is freedom to me."

Mercy stood and poured water into the basin then washed the tears from her face. Next she let her hair down. "Sometimes this hair gives me a headache. I'm tempted to cut it."

"Don't! I mean I rarely see it cascading down your back like that. It's beautiful, Mercy. It's not just blond, there are colors of a lighter brown and even a bit of red in it. It makes you look so—"

"Womanly?" She tossed her head so her hair moved.

"That word works, but I was going to say so very beautiful."

She pulled it all over one shoulder. "It's full of mud," she said smiling.

He stood and walked over to her and touched her hair. "Silky with a hint of mud. Mud is a given in this place."

GREG

Gently putting he put his arms around her and pulled her close. He swooped down and placed his lips against hers.

It always surprised her how his masculine lips were so soft when they kissed. She opened her mouth to him, and he deepened the kiss arousing longing inside her. It felt different somehow, as though they're hearts were both involved. Greg kissed her jaw and then her shoulder while she wrapped her arms around his neck. His hard chest pressed against hers and instead of being shocked she found she liked being so close to him. Their hips pressed together for a moment and then he stepped back.

He stared into her eyes. "I don't want to do anything you don't. If you're not ready tell me now."

"I think I'm falling in love with you. But there is so much I haven't figured out yet. You make me feel things I've never felt. When you touch me all thought goes out of my head. What if you decide you made a mistake come morning? My pa said that's how it is with most men." She bit her lip and glanced away.

"I'm not most men. I'm your husband. But I understand."

"No, go ahead do what you wanted to do."

Greg grinned and then laughed. "I will when we both want to do it. Longing is a powerful thing."

"I think that's what I felt." She met his gaze, and he nodded.

"That's a start. Let's get some sleep."

She nodded.

CHAPTER SIX

Greg woke and then stretched, hoping to work out the kinks on his back. He'd insisted they sleep in her bunk. At first it was nice and comfortable to have her in his arms but she moved a lot in her sleep and she kept her gun loaded under her pillow. He'd spent quite a bit of time praying it wouldn't go off.

He gazed down at her, thinking she reminded him of a sweet angel. She didn't have night clothes, so they slept in their regular clothes. He was just thankful she believed in cleanliness. Most of the miners stunk to high heaven.

He grabbed the pail and went to the pump for some fresh water. Most of the men he passed greeted him by name, and he nodded back at them. Then he went into their living quarters and poured some water into the wash basin. Next, he took off his shirt and retrieved his soap out of his saddlebag. He washed and then used some tooth powder. It was well past time to take a bath and wash his clothes.

He put the coffee on and opened the flap, keeping an eye on the camp activity. It was early for most miners. Especially the ones who spent what little they made down at Carl's place. He trotted out Shelly as the lure since she was clean and pretty. The rest of his ladies were filthy, and he was sure they probably had diseases they passed along to the miners.

His pa had warned him about women like that. His heart squeezed. He missed his family. As soon as they were finished mining, he was taking Mercy home to meet his ma and pa. They'd like her.

A groan came from beneath Mercy's blanket, and he knew she was up. Mornings were not her best time of day. It took her a while to fully wake. Coffee was a must for her. He poured it and handed it to her as soon as she swung her legs over the side of the bunk.

"How'd you sleep?" he asked.

"I think I was up all night. I'm not used to someone in my bunk." Her brows came together as she shook her head.

"Don't worry, you slept."

"How can you be so sure?" She stared at him.

"I know because I was up most of the night. You move constantly in your sleep. And I have to say your loaded gun under your pillow made me nervous. I was half afraid it'd go off."

"Ah, I was restless. That doesn't make for good sleep." She sipped her coffee. "I need to wash up."

Greg picked up the basin and threw the dirty water out of the tent. He then poured fresh water for her, grabbed her flowery soap, and placed it next to the basin. "I'll just step outside. I was thinking later we could wash clothes."

"We can do that."

He stood outside for what seemed like an awfully long time, but when he saw her it was worth the wait. Her hair was wet but she had braided it so it hung over her right shoulder.

"You look as pretty as a sunset in June."

She smiled as she turned a delightful shade of pink.

"Here comes Mac. We can go eat breakfast together." The surprise on her face put a grin on his. "I figured if people didn't see us together, then how'd they know we're married?"

"Good morning, Mac," she greeted.

"That it is," he replied.

They hurried down to the cook tent and greeted Ima. As they sat on one of the rough benches and ate, all the whispers and looks didn't go unnoticed. Greg took the opportunity to hold Mercy's hand whenever possible, and he kissed her right before they left.

"Goodness," Mercy said. "You'd think by the hoots and hollers they'd never seen married people kiss before." Her lovely shade of pink had deepened to a fiery red.

Greg took her hand. "They're just jealous is all. Let's mine for a while."

She kept glancing at him the whole way back. "Greg?"

"Yes?"

"Now it's just an idea but maybe we could make arrangements with the bath house owner for privacy."

"I bet with enough money anything can be arranged."

"I don't want to spend—"

"We have enough flake for a bath."

"True, flakes aren't nuggets." She smiled at Mac as she went into the mine.

Greg thanked Mac and was soon right behind her, stepping carefully over the cans. They removed the wood they had placed over the gold, and he couldn't help but marvel at it.

"Remember, we need just as much ordinary rock as gold. We have to be seen trying to examine the rocks in the sun and then throwing them in our pile in disgust." Mercy told him with excitement in her voice.

"I'll get the rocks, you be careful with the gold," Greg said. He took his pail and before he grabbed his pickaxe, he pulled

Mercy to him and gave her a long kiss. The dazed look in her eyes when he stopped was good for his ego.

MERCY USED A SMALLER pick to get the gold while he swung away with the large one. Soon enough she took the bucket with the rocks outside to pretend to examine them, and then she discarded them. She shook her head and asked other miners who walked by if they'd had any luck or if they thought the site was played out.

Most said they hadn't found much, just enough to continue to eat and keep mining. A few looked dumbstruck about the mine being played out. Most of the men were probably much younger than they looked. Some were hunched over and most had dust settled into the fine lines on their faces plus mud on their clothes. There weren't many smiles.

She wanted to jump up and shout her happiness. Not necessarily about the gold but about the soul-searing kiss her husband had given her last night and the one at the cook tent for everyone to see. He was a good man. He could be gentle and talk sweet, but he could also stare down an enemy and he wasn't afraid to use his gun.

It was good that she stopped them from going any further last night. Her father's words of morning regrets played in her mind. She had to be sure.

"Drinking up all the sunshine?"

She jumped, startled by her husband. She'd been so deep in thought she hadn't heard him come up behind her. That wasn't a good thing. She needed her wits about her.

"It's a nice change from the dark mine. I'm tired of rock and more rock. I'm beginning to believe that gold is a fools dream," she said loud enough for all those watching the couple to hear.

"I'm new at this, so I don't know how much a person needs to dig to find anything. Tell you what, why don't we wait another week or two and see if anything shows." He sat down next to her, picked up a rock and pretended to examine it. "I know it seems crazy gathering rocks day after day but I don't plan to go on to another mine after this. I'm heading home."

Her stomach dropped. Greg had told her he was eventually going home. She just hadn't counted on it being so soon. She'd been fascinated by his stories of how wonderful his family was, and sure, he'd mentioned taking her with him, staying her husband. But in her heart, she knew there was no place for a miner's rat there. The only thing she had going for her was her ability to read. She could sign her name, but writing wasn't something her Pa'd had time for. Greg deserved a wife he could be proud to bring home.

She stood and brushed some of the dirt from her trousers. "I'll go gather another bucket full of rocks." She slipped back down into the mine and leaned against the wall, waiting for her heart beat to slow. She'd need to make her own plan. She'd had dreams of being her own woman. A business owner perhaps, but now she needed a solid plan.

She gathered rocks and filled her bucket. Fatigue crept up on her, and she slowly dragged the bucket out of the mine. She was coming out as Greg was going back in. "Put it on the bottom and top it off with rocks and leave it near the fire."

"Why not hide it?"

"The best place to hide something is in plain sight." She didn't wait for a response but went back outside and sat down. So much had happened in the last few weeks. They'd struck gold, her pa was dead, she was now married, and she'd killed a man. And so much more. A near hanging and kisses. It was a lot to take in.

There was a hole in her heart left by her pa's death. This was his dream and he hadn't lived to enjoy it. He could have been set for life. She was adrift with no place to be. She never did ask Greg if he had a sweetheart waiting for him at home. She watched Shelly standing out front of the saloon tent. That was what a man wanted, a pretty woman who could laugh and make a man feel good about himself.

It wouldn't be fair to make Greg have to tell her she wasn't a real wife. She needed to leave before he did. She could travel to one town, get cleaned up and buy some pretty dresses and then decide her future. After that she'd travel to a new town and start a new life. It really didn't sound so difficult. Except for the part where she'd have to leave Greg. She wouldn't even be able to write him a note telling why she'd left.

She watched the whole camp while she supposedly looked at the rocks. Many miners left the camp amid celebration because they'd struck color, only to find themselves victims on the way to the bank to cash in. Some snuck out in the middle of the night, only to be accosted because their actions made them look suspicious. But the ones who pulled out without hitting gold, usually left in disgrace and as far as she knew, none were assaulted along the trail out. She and Greg needed to leave like those miners. But they would need a better wagon and team since Greg had traded for a mule. If she couldn't arrange a trade without drawing attention to them, she was going to have to steal a wagon and team. But from which man? Which of these yahoos was green and would be easily talked into trading a team and wagon for a mule? Someone who was new would be the easiest to pretend to befriend.

Finally, she made her decision. There was a miner named

GREG

Tim two claims down, and he always wore an expression of confusion. He was a bit shy and didn't often ask questions. Yes, he would be her new friend. Well, hers and Greg's, and she'd make sure to compensate him somehow when they left. Plus it wasn't really using him; she'd give him enough pointers to make the trade more than even.

Greg plopped down next to her and stretched his legs out in front of him. "I'm bushed. I thought swinging the pickaxe was hard work but hauling those heavy good-for-nothing rocks is a real killer." He took a deep breath and stood up. "I have an errand to run. I'll be back to get you."

She drew her brows together as she watched him walk down the hill. The promised bath! She hoped he could make it happen. Meanwhile, she went back in and gathered her towel and soap and did the same for him.

GREG ENJOYED Mercy's smile the whole way to the bathhouse tent. It had cost him dearly but he wanted to do something to make her happy. They walked in and there were men, naked men enjoying their baths. He quickly steered Mercy to the other side of the tent, where blankets had been hung for her privacy.

Her eyes widened. The tub was large and she walked closer to it. "It's new water!" She quickly began to undress then stopped and stared at him. If you plan to stand guard, you'll have to turn around."

He was glad he insisted on a clean tub and water. The usual practice was for many men to bathe in the same water until it was so dirty you couldn't see the bottom of the tub. And there was a ten minute time limit. He listened as she removed her clothes, only able to imagine what she looked like. His longing for her grew anew, and he had to keep his groans to himself. It never occurred to him just how uncomfortable the situation would be.

He heard the quiet slosh of water as she stepped into the tub and sat. Her satisfied sigh washed over him, heating him from the inside. Was her hair down? Was her body all rosy from the warm water? Water slashed and he imagined her washing herself. She was probably lathering her soap and spreading it on herself.

"Is it warm enough?" he asked, eager for her to be happy with the bath.

"It's heavenly, and my muscles feel like they are relaxing. Did you get the ten minute bath? How long have I been in here?" Her voice sounded breathless and sexy.

"We have half an hour. I figured twenty minutes for you and ten for me." Too bad he couldn't see her face. Was she surprised? Pleased?

"Well that hardly seems fair. We should each get fifteen minutes," she murmured.

There was more splashing. Was she washing her hair now? Did it shroud her body? His body tensed as a chill rolled through him. Why had he thought this would be a good idea? It was an exercise in torture. Closing his eyes he could remember the feel of her soft body against his when he'd kissed her.

"Oh no!"

He started to turn but stopped in time. "What's going on?"

"I need my towel. I got soap in my eyes. I left it out of reach. I'll get out and get it."

"No. Where is it?"

"On the stool. I guess I wasn't thinking about anything but the hot water. If you take five steps back you'll be next to the stool."

How was he going to do this without peeking at her? He

walked back five steps and his foot hit the stool. Both of their towels were on it. He grabbed hers and reached behind him.

"Just turn real quick and hand it to me and try not to look." She sounded nervous.

"Sure." He turned and handed her the towel but there was nothing quick about it. Her hair fully covered one rounded breast but he got more than a glimpse of the other one. She must have thought both were covered because she didn't try to use her hands to hide her nakedness. He didn't dare try to look into the water. He'd seen more than enough to make him want her with great need. He handed her the towel and turned away.

No more baths for them, at least not at the same time. He couldn't do this again. His natural urge was to lift her from the water and kiss her, and it was near impossible to keep from acting on his urges.

"I'm glad I had saved a clean set of clothes. I would have hated putting on the dirty ones. Are you all right? I'm getting out, and if we both turn our backs we won't see a thing. You can get undressed while I get dressed."

He took a deep breath and let it out slowly. "Sounds like a plan." He waited until she was wrapped in her towel and told him it was fine for him to start undressing. He was glad she couldn't see him. He'd probably scare her. He had no idea what she knew of the male anatomy.

Greg turned his head and grabbed his own soap, and his mouth went dry at the sight of her delectable backside. He quickly turned away. No more looking, his body couldn't handle any more. He concentrated on getting the dirt off of him.

Then he climbed into the water. It was still fairly warm. And it smelled like her soap. Oh, lawdy. He tried holding his breath, but that wasn't going to work.

"Doesn't it feel wonderful?" she asked, her voice sounded so happy.

"It sure does," he answered in a tight voice. "Ah…you can go back to the mine if you like. You don't have to wait for me."

"I wouldn't think of it. I'll wait for you."

Shivers rippled through him, and they had nothing to do with the cooling water. He washed, dried himself, and got dressed in record time. When he was ready to leave, he took her hand and led her out of the tent. Gulping in the fresh air helped him some.

She smiled at him. "I forgot to tell you. I figured out a way to get us out of here without folks knowing about…it."

"Oh?"

"It involves being friends with one of the miners, but it'll be worth it."

"What kind of friends? Friends like Shelly is to miners?"

She snatched her hand from his and stalked off.

Dang it! Greg wanted to kick himself. The words had just come out. He never once thought of Mercy that way. What was wrong with him? Spending too much time knowing she'd had her clothes off was what was wrong, and he'd just taken it out on her. He had some apologizing to do.

MERCY STOPPED at Tim's claim. It seemed that most miners didn't have last names, or at least never went by them. It had always amused her in the past, but she had no reason to be amused at the moment.

"I just wanted to introduce myself to you. It might not look like it, but I've been mining most of my life with my father. You were probably here when he died."

GREG

Tim nodded. He was tall and incredibly thin with light brown hair that needed cutting. "I was sorry to hear about it."

She clasped her hands in front of her. "If you need anything I'm two claims away."

She felt the heat of Greg's body behind her and stiffened, but she didn't turn around.

"I'm Greg, Mercy's husband." He held out his hand and shook hands with Tim. "Really if you need anything, Mercy is the one to ask. It was nice to meet you." He put his arm around her waist and led her away.

"Don't touch me," she hissed as quietly as possible.

He removed his arm from around her but continued walking beside her. He didn't say a word, and that unnerved her. He should be begging her forgiveness instead of acting as though he hadn't compared her to Shelly.

Mercy walked faster until she was in the living quarters. She faced the wooden wall and tried to stem the tears that threatened. She wasn't some silly girl that cried. Really, she wasn't. She crossed her arms in front of her and bowed her head. The bath had been so incredibly wonderful, and then he'd said those ugly words. He wasn't the man she had thought him to be. Disappointment poured over her. It didn't matter. She planned to leave him anyway.

She breathed deeply. Somehow it did matter, a great deal according to the breaking of her heart. She thought about the conversation, but no, there was no mistaking what he meant.

"Why?" she asked.

"I don't know. I'm sorrier than I can express."

"You're my husband," she whispered trying not to cry but tears started to flow down her face. She felt him walk behind her.

"I don't think I can explain it to someone as innocent as you," he said his voice seemed to be full of sorrow.

Mercy turned around. "It didn't sound as though you

thought me to be innocent a little bit ago. Greg, you compared me to Shelly. I'm nothing like her, nothing. I don't understand any of this. You find a way to get us out of here in secret. I'm done."

"You did talk to Tim. I'm sure you have it all figured out."

Her jaw dropped. "Yes, I did talk to him. Despite what you said, I still thought it the best way. I knew you were wrong in your thinking, and I believed that was all that mattered, but to my utter dismay you've hurt me." She sat down on her bunk and wiped away her tears but there was no way to keep up with them. "How? I thought…" She stared at the fire. "I think it best if you slept elsewhere tonight. I'd like to be alone."

She heard the flap move, and when she looked up she was alone. So much for sparing his feelings when she left. She'd have to leave much sooner than she thought. She was no good at pretending to like someone when in her heart she hated him. If he'd just said he didn't want a wife it still would have hurt, she realized, but not as bad as being compared to a whore.

She got her scale out along with all her hidden nuggets and set about weighing them. She had enough to leave. Not enough to start a new life but enough to feed herself and find lodging for a while. She put everything back and lay on her bunk. If she could hold out for a few days she'd have enough. It would be like selling her soul, but it would be her best bet.

Exhaustion hit her. "Pa, why did you leave me?" Tears still poured as she lay there. It was good that they never consummated the wedding. Greg would have certainly have had morning regrets. Well, a few more days and she'd be gone.

CHAPTER SEVEN

Greg sat outside his tent and watched the sun rise. Sleep had been elusive. He wasn't the type to try to hurt a woman, but he had. The remark about Shelly had come out from jealousy. He didn't want her to talk to any other miner. But she had done it anyway. Perhaps she was too headstrong for her own good. Did she even think before she acted? She needed his protection, and whether she agreed or not, she was getting it.

He stood and went to their mine. He opened the flap and grabbed the bucket. As he walked to get water he got many knowing looks. Everyone seemed to know he and Mercy had had a fight.

"Got on her bad side, did you?" Mac asked as he stepped alongside Greg.

"You know how women are."

Mac grunted. "You were gentle weren't you? Women like gentle."

Greg furrowed his brow. "Gentle?"

"When you were, well…in the bathhouse. You were

taking your time and not rutting, right?" A dark shade of red crept into Mac's face.

"So everyone thinks I was rough with my wife in the bathhouse?" He tried to keep his voice calm, but he didn't manage to do it.

"We all saw you two go in and the next thing we know you're sleeping back at your claim. We came to the conclusion you did something wrong." He scratched his chin and shrugged. "Sweet talking helps."

"We were having a disagreement about something else. She's used to mining and not seeing gold. I'm all for moving on, but she thinks it would be wiser to stay." Greg gave him a sidelong look. He relaxed when Mac nodded.

Greg filled his bucket and skedaddled back to the mine. He walked in and found Mercy up and dressed, pulling her mud-caked boots on. When she was finished, she grabbed the dipper and took some water, poured it into her tin cup, and then drank it down. She wiped her mouth with her sleeve and walked into the mine.

He'd had the silent treatment from his sisters before. It wouldn't last long. After putting coffee on, he grabbed his gloves and a lamp and then went down into the mine. Mercy had already removed the boards covering the vein of gold. Her body stiffened when he joined her, but she didn't turn to look at him.

Fine with him, he'd use the pickaxe and get enough rocks to fool everyone. He swung once then twice. It felt great to get his anger out as he hit more rock. The whole camp thought he'd been a buffoon when making love to his wife. He wouldn't know, and at the rate they were going he'd never know. It was crazy. She was his wife; she should be doing what wives did.

He almost laughed. She didn't know what wives did. She didn't know how a lady acted. She'd grown up with miners

GREG

and acted like one. He filled the pail with rocks and went back to fresh air.

He sat outside and examined a rock. He wasn't being fair to Mercy. She was a kind, gentle, caring woman, and he was lucky to have her. Somehow he'd have to convince her he cared about her.

Greg watched as Carl was making the rounds. He did it every day to remind those who owed him money that he'd take their claim in satisfaction. He really meant he'd take it by force. Carl started to walk by without a second glance at Greg.

"Carl, can I ask you something?" Greg asked.

"What can I do for you? I hear you and Mercy are on the outs. Shelly is good at consoling men." His face twisted into an ugly leer.

"Mercy and I are married. We'll get it figured out. Why would you take worthless mines as payment for a debt? It doesn't seem like good business to me."

Carl pushed his hat back on his head. "That's why I'm a businessman and you're a miner. There have been a few smaller strikes around here. If I own enough of the claims I'll talk one of the mining companies to come in and dig this whole place up. They usually build a town of sorts and bring their own men. Now these men get mighty thirsty and needy."

"You've done this before."

Carl nodded. "If you can be one step ahead of the companies, you can make good money. One day, I'll find a town I want to settle in, and I'll build myself the biggest house and have the prettiest wife."

Greg stared at him. "No one else is trying to do the same thing?"

Carl's grin turned evil. "If they do, they soon find out it

isn't good for their health." He took a menacing step toward Greg. "Understand?"

"Sure, I understand. Could you take a look at this rock? It seems prettier than the others. Is it anything?" He handed the rock to Carl.

Carl frowned and then laughed. "That ain't no gold. You keep trying though. You never know you might strike it rich."

He released a heavy sigh. "Darn, I was hoping."

"You don't know what it looks like?" Carl asked.

"Not on a rock. I've seen a couple nuggets miners have, but that's it."

Carl shrugged. "Maybe you should mine your claim and let Mercy mine this one. Your tent could be sitting on a wagonload of gold." Shaking his head, Carl walked away.

It felt good to fool Carl. Now he thought Greg to be stupid, and that was just fine. And he'd found out why Carl wanted the claims. Greg planned to be far away from the mining camp before it became a town. He was so lost in thought he didn't notice Mercy until she blocked the sun.

She sat next to him and was silent for a while. Finally she turned to him. "What rock did you show him?"

Greg handed it to her.

"I do believe that to be quartz. You're a good liar. Carl won't be watching you as closely anymore."

A good liar? He didn't think she meant it as a compliment. "I'm sorry about yesterday."

She looked out at the camp. "You aren't usually so mean. I'm not used to being compared to a whore."

"Mercy, look at me." He waited until she turned her head. In the sunlight he could see how puffy her eyes were, and his heart hurt. "I didn't mean to be such a jerk. I didn't realize listening to you bathe would make me so crazy."

"I don't know what you mean."

He nodded. "I know, and that's the problem. I'm wildly

attracted to you, and my body responds to the thought of us in bed together."

"But we sleep in the same bunk, well except for last night." Her eyes widened. "You want—oh, my. That's why you mentioned Shelly. I couldn't figure out why you said what you did because I've never—"

He reached out and took her hand. "I know you haven't. Do you ever think about it or feel desire?"

Mercy quickly jumped up and went into the living quarters.

Greg sighed and followed her. "Mercy, I'm sorry if I embarrassed you."

"I thought there was something wrong with me. You didn't seem to want me, and I felt like a hussy. My heart can feel the pull of your heart. But unless you plan to stay my husband, I'd rather we left things the way they are. I don't want to be left carrying your baby. It's a lot to think about." Her eyes looked determined though a bit misty. "I'm going back in."

He watched her leave. Why did she think he was leaving her? It seemed from the first she'd never thought of them as really married.

FOR THE NEXT week Mercy slept in her bunk alone while Greg slept in her father's. They did the same thing each day. She'd mine the gold while he broke pieces of rock from the walls of the mine. Each day she'd hide the gold under the commode and then late in the day, they'd sit outside together pretending to examine rocks.

Finally, one night Mercy finally saw Tim leave his claim. She snuck in and stole two of the large empty crates she'd caught a glimpse of when she had first talked to him. She shifted some of his belongings and moved a couple of other supply crates around to cover what she'd taken. Her heart beat wildly until she was once again safe at her mine. She sat on her bunk smiling at a job well done.

SHE SMILED as she grabbed some smaller pieces of lumber and cut them to fit in the bottom of the crates. When she was satisfied with the fit, she took the lumber out and laid it aside. Finally, she grabbed the hidden gold. Using the small pick, she broke some of the dirt away from the vein of gold. Then she layered the gold into the bottom of the crate and set the lumber on top of it, creating a false bottom. She added a blanket and then searched the living quarters for more goods to set inside the crate. A cleanish shirt that had been her pa's covered more of the bottom. She tested the weight of the crate. It was fairly heavy. With another glance around, her gaze lit on some tin plates and matching cups. She added those to the top, along with a frame that had belonged to her ma. Satisfied that they would be able to lift the crate, she turned to the next and fashioned its false bottom.

GREG WANDERED in as she was laying the gold inside, and his eyes grew wide. He took his gun out of his holster. "I'll stand by the entrance. You're not making those too heavy?"

SHE SHOOK her head and studied the finished false bottom. "I think they'll be manageable, but I'll need to make more false bottoms on some of our other crates.

GREG

She settled more gold in the bottom of the crate and laid lumber over the pieces. It fit even better than the first. She laid in more of her father's clothing then left room at the top for work tools.

She exchanged grins with Greg. It looked like her idea might work. They could leave in disgrace, appearing broke and ready to give up with no one the wiser. She reburied the gold that hadn't fit in the two crates. She wanted to celebrate. Success like this was why so many men yelled "Eureka!" when they struck gold. It was a life changer. It was validation of all the hardships and hard work. She just stood in the middle of the living quarters and smiled. They were going to do it.

Greg peeked outside once again before he holstered his gun. He smiled back but he didn't move.

Mercy sighed. They hadn't made any steps to become closer to each other. She tried to ignore him half the time. She wasn't sure what she expected but one thing she knew for sure he should make the first move. She honestly thought he'd try to reassure her that he wasn't leaving her behind but he never said a word about it. It was plain to her that he too didn't think of their marriage as real.

Prospecting for gold left too much time to dream and it hurt to dream because all her dreams included him. He'd go back to Oregon and perhaps she'd go to San Francisco. She'd never see him again. Her happiness flowed away.

"How long before we can go?"

"I have to figure out how to get Tim to trade us for his wagon," she murmured. "I don't want to cheat him, but if we pay him in gold, our secret will be out."

"You don't trust him?" asked Greg, frowning.

"He's green. I don't know if he can keep his mouth shut.

Their gazes met and held.

"How much can we take? I don't think it smart to cash the gold in anywhere near here. Instead of trusting Tim, I'll go and get us an old wagon and a team." He rubbed the back of his head. "Something kinda beat up, like someone down on his luck might be able to purchase.

"Will I be riding on that wagon, too?"

"If that's what you want, Mercy. I know you have plans that don't include me, but I thought we'd go and stay with my parents for a bit. They'll love you." His voice was gentle.

"You don't have to feel responsible for me. I can take care of myself." She went and sat on her bunk and stared into the fire. She already felt the ache of losing him. The pain would only worsen. Her heart was going to break no matter what she did. Why not take the comfort he offered now? She'd never find another man she loved like she loved Greg.

She turned and studied his face. His strong jaw always fascinated her. "You can come to my bunk if you wish."

He stared at her as though he'd never seen her before, and her face heated. Why hadn't she just kept her mouth shut?

"Mercy, are you coming with me when I leave?" He was so serious as though this was the question that would determine their lives.

Time went by, and silence filled the small living quarters while she tried to figure out what to say. She took too long, and he shook his head and left. Perhaps it was better that he

GREG

did leave. She'd give anything to have him holding her again but he didn't want her. Not really. He'd find out as soon as she was among people other than miners that she didn't know how to behave. She wasn't one to mix with polite society, and she was hopelessly inadequate.

Heck, she didn't even have proper clothes. If she went her own way, she could buy the clothes and not have to mingle with others. She'd hire a girl who could do all errands and she'd be the woman who never came out of her house. But it would be a fine house. She lay down on her bunk. It would also be a lonely house with no husband and no children, but that would be better than being a constant embarrassment to Greg.

She tossed and turned until Greg stumbled through the flap and flopped down on his bunk. She could smell the whiskey on his breath.

She also could smell perfume.

It shook her to her core, and she tried everything to keep the tears at bay, but they wouldn't be denied. She cried silently into her pillow.

She could break some of the larger rock with color into smaller pieces, take some of the better ones. A saddle bag filled with some would be enough. She could take them and be on her way. First she'd need a ride to Hang Town so she could catch a coach to San Francisco. She had enough smaller nuggets to use to buy what she needed. She didn't want to be robbed. She'd inquire starting tomorrow.

GREG WOKE UP AND GROANED. He wasn't much of a drinker, but knowing that Mercy didn't love him had beat him up inside. He had thought he'd have a drink then go back, but Carl had bought him a couple more. He hoped Mercy had been asleep before he returned. He remembered most of the night, but some things were a bit hazy.

He sat up feeling better than he'd imagined. The flap was open, and he could see by the position of the sun that he'd missed most of the morning. It didn't matter how much he loved her, he couldn't make Mercy love him back. Maybe he was only lovable to his ma.

He washed and drank some coffee before he went into the mine. From the glare he received, he gathered Mercy had been awake when he came in last night.

"I'm sorry, I got up late."

She still glared.

"I had a few whiskeys, and I'm not one for drinking much. It clouded my thinking."

"Who did you tell about the mine?"

He furrowed his brow. "No one. Why? Was someone here?"

"No one sweet talked information from you?"

"Why would you think that?" Alarm shot through him. "Mercy, did something happen?"

"If you don't remember, maybe you should have a talk with Shelly. You came in with whiskey on your breath and Shelly's perfume on you. The perfume was very strong, so you must have spent a lot of close time together," she said in a sad voice. "Well, I have work to do. "I hid more gold in the corner there, under those heavier rocks." She turned and continued to mine the gold.

He swallowed hard as he grabbed the pickaxe. He drove the tool into the wall over and over, struggling to remember Shelly and last night. He recalled her being there, but he would swear he hadn't touched her. She'd sat on his lap more than once and put her hand on his arm while whispering invitations to go upstairs to him. He hadn't gone. And he didn't tell anyone about the gold.

GREG

He kept at it until he had enough rocks in the bucket. Then he put down the pickaxe and went to Mercy's side. "I didn't lie with Shelly. I respect the vows we took, you and I, and I'd never endanger you by talking about the mine."

He grabbed the bucket and walked outside. Her eyes had grown big and round. They were also red, he'd noticed, even in the dim light. Once again, he had caused her pain. He needed to figure out what to do to make her smile again. He hadn't a clue. His pa would have known for sure. But his pa was far away in Oregon. He sat outside and pretended to examine the rocks. It was boring work.

Catching movement in the corner of his eye, he watched as Glad made his way up to the mine. "Hey, Glad."

"Howdy. Listen, I have something for you to give to your wife. I figured you'd be on the outs today after last night."

"Truthfully, Glad, last night was a bit of a blur."

Glad sat down next to him. "Heck, they plied you with whiskey and kept asking if your mine had any gold. They even asked you to sign the mine over. I should say mines, they wanted both of them. When that didn't work, they got Shelly to have a go at you."

Greg's heart beat frantically as he started questioning the way he had remembered things. "I didn't?"

"Naw, you pushed her off you more than once. She tried sitting on your lap and kissing your neck. You wanted no part of her. Her and Carl were hoppin' mad when you left. They wasted free whiskey and Shelly's attention on you, and you didn't oblige them. I've seen it work for them more times than not, but not last night. Anyway, I figured your wife was probably pretty hurt. Shelly wears so much perfume that anyone she touches goes back smelling like her."

"That's the truth. I don't know what to say to Mercy," Greg confessed.

"Here." Glad handed Greg a wedding band. "I made this a

long time ago. I was going to give it to my wife, but she took off."

"I can't take this. She might be back."

Glad shook his head. "She knows where I am if she needs me. I can make another one. I like makin' them."

"Let me at least pay you."

Glad stood up. "It's my wedding present to you both. You're wasting your time with those rocks. I doubt any of them have a speck of gold."

Greg stood and shook Glad's hand. "Thank you. You're probably right about the rocks, but anything is better than nothing."

Greg closed his hand around the ring. He needed to have a talk with Mercy. He wanted her in his life. But she sure was a stubborn woman, and his behavior last night hadn't helped anything."

A SUPPLY WAGON came at least once a week, always on Wednesdays and sometimes on Saturdays. She'd best plan to leave next Wednesday. She groaned as she mined the gold. Today was Thursday. It would be a long heart breaking week. But at least he hadn't told anyone about the gold. The rest didn't matter.

She took a deep breath, but the heartache was worse than ever. Maybe she should have asked him to bed her. He probably figured out she just wasn't meant to be a wife. Why else go with Shelly? If only she had a place to hide from everyone. The house in San Francisco she'd dreamed up was sounding better and better. She needed her pa. He'd have known what to do. Her heart twisted. She still expected him to come walking into the mine like he always did.

The more gold they could mine the better. She wanted

enough to get away with, but Greg deserved an equal share. The vein of gold they'd found hadn't petered out, and she didn't expect it to. She chipped away at the gold faster than before. She needed as much as she could possibly carry. She could take the mule. She'd be able put gold in the saddle bags. She could also carry some. Then once in town she could buy a horse. Taking a stage coach was out after all. People would know by the weight, what she was carrying. She'd need to start gathering supplies.

Things were getting complicated. Maybe she should go in the same direction as Greg. There was bound to be a town near his family's ranch. It would be the smarter option, but could her heart take it? If loving meant so much heartache, she'd rather not love. Caring too much just led to unhappiness. She wanted her calm life back. Not that it had been really calm. They'd always been moving, but she had known what to expect. With Greg, she was out of her element. And he deserved better.

She gathered the gold, half-filled a bucket, and threw plain rocks on top. Then she went at it again. Now that she had changed her plan, she needed the gold as quick as possible so they could leave and then go their own ways.

Finally, she had two buckets full. Where was Greg? He must be done pretending to examine the haul of rocks he'd taken outside. Shrugging she grabbed one bucket and headed up. There was Greg sitting on his bunk seemingly deep in thought. He hadn't noticed her. That wasn't like him.

She put the pail down and sat down next to him. "Did something happen? Did you get some bad news?"

He blinked a few times before he turned and gazed at her. "I guess I have a lot on my mind, and I want to talk to you about it. That is, if we're even talking."

Her stomach clenched. "Yes we can talk." She took a deep breath and let it out slowly, waiting for him to start.

He took her hand and entwined their fingers. "I'm sorry as can be about my behavior last night. I was hurt, but drinking never solved anything. I understand you want to go your own way. You've been pretty independent your whole life, and you have no need for a husband. I just wish I had figured that out before I came to care for you. If you want to stay here, that's fine, or I could help you get to wherever you plan to go. If you even want help, that is."

He drew a shaky breath. "Glad stopped by, and he was at the saloon last night. He told me they plied me with whiskey in the hope that it would cause trouble between us or that maybe I'd sign our claims away. I'm not exactly sure what the plan was, but they threw Shelly at me too, and I didn't take what was offered."

He paused and looked outside. "We need—I need to know where I stand with you. I can't keep hoping if there is no hope. You've said it before, we never consummated the marriage, so technically we could walk away from each other."

Her body stiffened as her heart dropped. This was it. She wouldn't need a plan, Greg would make sure she got to where she wanted to go. She could live alone. Only thing was…somehow it didn't seem appealing anymore.

"Is that what you want?" she asked not wanting the answer.

"No." His voice was very soft. "I don't want to walk away, and I'm hoping you don't either. What we have here is a once in a lifetime find. Do you agree?"

Did he mean their marriage or the gold? "Once in a lifetime, yes it is." She glanced away. "Does this mean you want to stay together?"

"I think it's best for both of us."

She glanced back at him. Where was the declaration of love? Where were the sweet words?

"I have something for you." He let go of her hand and fished in his pocket. He handed her a gold ring. "This is for you."

"A wedding ring?" she asked cautiously. She didn't want to read more into it than it was.

"Yes, Glad made it. Put it on, let's see if it fits."

She nodded. Greg wasn't even smiling. She slid it onto her finger, and it was a good fit. "It's beautiful, thank you. I didn't know Glad was so talented. Did you ask him to make it?"

"Naw, he had it in his pocket, hoping his wife would come back but so far she hasn't, so he thought I could use it to give to you." He smiled. "He's a good guy."

She tried her hardest to smile, but she knew it must have looked fake. "Thank you. It's a good thing he had one in his pocket."

Greg nodded. "He knew you'd be upset about how many times Shelly tried to persuade me to go upstairs with her."

She stood. "I'm going to see if Ima has any tea. Thank Glad for me." She hurried down the hill, but she didn't go into the cook tent. She followed the stream for a while. It must have been a beautiful place before the miners came. She found a big flat rock and sat on it. The feel of the warm sun was a comfort.

Was she too sensitive? Did she expect too much? If she understood Greg correctly, he didn't ask for a ring, Glad offered him one to soften the fact that Shelly had spent her whole time with Greg. The ring was nice, and Glad had a talent. He was also the thoughtful one who seemed to care about her feelings. Or maybe not. Maybe he just wanted his friend, Greg to get into her good graces.

She didn't know enough about men, but it seemed to her that Greg didn't care as much as Glad did. At least Greg had a friend. The loneliness inside her was becoming unbearable.

She hadn't observed many marriages. Perhaps this was just the way of things, but she'd thought it would be different. She thought they'd grow to be close. She'd thought they'd be happy.

It was mortifying to know Greg hadn't asked for the ring. He had probably never considered getting her one. So the ring was really from Glad, not her husband. Her hopes and expectations were too high. She needed to take them down to the very bottom, or she was going to spend her days being hurt.

Her pa had always talked about her mother with love in his voice and in his eyes. He'd missed her a great deal. And Mercy had always hoped… But it was time to grow up and put her childish hopes and dreams away. Greg was offering friendship, wasn't he? He said he cared for her. She was too confused to really know what he wanted. She'd need him to get all the gold away from the mine. She jumped down off the rock and walked back. She just hoped her heart could take it.

CHAPTER EIGHT

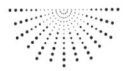

Three Weeks Later

Greg looked around their living quarters and made sure they had all their belongings packed. The only light to look with was the firelight. Despite Mercy's idea of leaving in broad daylight, they had decided to leave in the dead of night because it had seemed like Carl was paying them too much mind. It had been a long three weeks but they worked hard and they were ready to go.

With the help of Mac and Glad, they would get away, hopefully unnoticed. Greg had bought their wagon and loaded it a little at a time. Glad had driven it out for them as though heading to town to sell it, and he'd hidden it in a safe place for them to pick up on their way out. Greg and Mercy decided to give their claims to Mac and Glad to share. Once everything was explained, the two men were more than happy to help the couple get away.

Greg had asked just about everyone what San Francisco was like and how to get there. Mercy mentioned Texas all the time but also said that Greg had gold fever and she didn't think they'd ever settle down.

Shoving his hat on, Greg left the mine. He walked a great distance to where Mercy and Mac waited. Glad was going to immediately take possession of the two claims. It was getting a bit chilly at night and he was glad he'd worn his coat and he'd made Mercy wear hers too.

Mercy… He smiled. She could be ornery a lot of the time, but he wouldn't have chosen anyone else to have as a wife. He loved the way her eyes lit up when she was mad. Lately, she'd been plenty mad and he wasn't sure why. Things would get better as soon as they settled on his pa's property.

He found them all without difficulty, and when he got closer he could see the excitement dancing in Mercy's eyes. He shook Mac's hand and they quietly went on their way. It wasn't always the wisest thing to ride at night, but they'd picked a night where the moon would be full. Mac was to ride his mule in a few different directions in the hope that no one would be able to pick up their trail.

Greg and Mercy rode in almost circles for a bit, then they found the hidden wagon and set out for Oregon. They rode slow and steady all night long, only stopping to rest the animals. The sun came up, and they picked up the pace until rain clouds blew in and landed them in the middle of a storm.

"Do you want to find cover?" he yelled over the wind.

Mercy shook her head. "No, we need to keep going. I don't trust Carl not to come after us!" she called back.

Greg nodded. They'd be fine for the day but they'd need shelter and a fire in the evening. They'd be chilled through with wet clothes. They both scanned the area as they rode. They'd heard of bushwhackers and they didn't intend to become their victims.

Mercy pulled the wagon to a stop and pointed at a group of rocks. She nodded, and they both grabbed their rifles.

He motioned for her to hold the team as he slapped his

horse's hind flank. The riderless horse raced by the rocks. Three men stood up with their mouths open, looking around. But Greg had already slipped off into the woods and rounded until he was behind the men. Mercy kept behind the cover the wagon provided and waited.

"Looking for something?" Greg asked with his gun pointed at the men.

The youngest one pulled his gun and shot, missing Greg. Greg ducked behind a boulder and shot back. He heard a cry. Good, he'd gotten one. He figured they'd try to go around and get the jump on him. He waited and listened. The rain made it harder, but he was able to run and take cover before they began to shoot.

Splintered rock fell down on him. They were getting too close. Then he heard a rifle shot and saw one of the men fall all the way to the ground. The last man tried to run, but Greg shot him in the shoulder. He climbed to the man and took his gun.

There was a great amount of blood coming from the gunman's shoulder. "Who sent you?"

The young man turned white and shook his head. "No one. We heard you coming and we hid is all."

The man wasn't a very good liar.

"I'm asking again. Who sent you?" Greg pressed down on the wound until the man screamed."

"It was a man named Carl. I don't know his last name. We've been waiting two days for you to come."

"Any others that you know about?" Greg leaned over to press on the wound again.

"I'll tell you anything mister, just stop hurting me. No others this way. He has a gang waiting for you on the San Francisco trail. He said we'd all split the gold. One of the men you shot is his brother in law. He won't take kindly to that."

"Hopefully, he won't find us in Texas."

"No Texas was a ruse. Carl figured you two out. Amateurs, he called you."

"The joke is on him, we didn't find much gold. We're going to Texas to ranch." Greg turned and walked away.

"Hey! You can't leave me here!"

Greg kept walking. They'd best get more distance between them and Carl.

When he found Mercy, still holding the rifle, his heart swelled. His relief that she hadn't a scratch on her weakened him for a moment.

"We'll go on for a bit longer. We can shelter in the wagon, though it'll be cramped."

Mercy nodded and climbed onto the wagon. Greg's horse had come back to him, and he climbed on. Soon enough they were in the dense woods.

"It's so dark," Mercy called out.

"We'd best walk the horses. We wouldn't want them to step into any holes. Look for dry wood as we go. We'll need it."

She frequently pointed to fallen limb and dead branches, and he was impressed at how much wood she spotted. She smiled at him and gestured for him to look up. He smiled right back. She'd found a cave. They would be able to park the wagon next to the entrance, affording them a bit of extra cover.

"I'll go first to make sure it's clear of bears or wolves. It looks like we can walk up the slope on the other side of it." She was a great partner and a big help.

Greg grabbed his rifle and hiked up to the cave. It was black as a moonless night inside. He listened and didn't hear anything. Then he grabbed a match and lit it. It shed momentary light, and as far as he could see all was clear. He walked back down and led Mercy and the team hauling the wagon up the narrow path. It would be tricky getting back down,

GREG

but it was doable.

He took care of the animals and saw that Mercy had made a roaring fire.

"I could have gotten to that," he said. He put his hands on either side of her waist and leaned in. He kissed her, and somehow she left him breathless. She'd gotten the hang of kissing and then some. The firelight made her lips appear a bit swollen. Mercy looked like a woman made for loving.

Mercy turned from Greg and touched her lips. He made her whole body feel alive with just a kiss. She'd never heard of such a thing. Maybe he'd had a lot of practice. She walked to the fire and held her hands out to warm them.

"We'll need to change into dry clothes," he said.

She nodded. "I'll get them for us both. It would be nice to feel dry and warm again. This weather makes travel uncomfortable." She slipped to the back of the wagon and pulled bedding, clothing, and a towel from the old trunk that had always traveled with her and her pa. She grabbed a cooking pot on her way out. She handed Greg his. "I think it's dark enough if I step out of the fire light. I'll be right back."

She took her time getting undressed. Next, she dried herself off with the towel. She saw Greg peek in her direction a time or two, but she was confident he couldn't see her. It felt strange; she hardly ever stood anywhere entirely unclothed. But she could trust her husband, and that made her proud. He was a good man.

As soon as she was done she walked to the fire and relished the heat it gave. "Your turn."

He took his clothes and grinned. "No looking, now."

"I wouldn't dream of it." She rummaged through another bag and found a can of beans which she opened and poured into the pot. After she put it in some of the hot coals, she looked toward the back of the cave. Her jaw dropped.

Shaking her head she looked again. She could see every detail of his naked backside. Outrage grew inside her. The light made it farther than she had thought. When he'd peeked at her, he'd seen her in all her glory. Disappointment slammed through her. Her body was hers, and she planned to share it with him someday when they had their wedding night, not like this, with clandestine glances. Her face heated and she wasn't sure what to do. The rain pounded down harder.

She grabbed her bedroll and laid it out by the fire. It was a bit damp, but the fire would take care of it. She lay down with her back to him and pulled the blanket up over her. Her hands clenched and unclenched and her body was stiff. She listened and knew he'd come to the fire and was probably staring at her right now. She'd been such a fool to think him to be admirable. He probably only wanted her along to help haul the gold.

She tried to harden her heart, but her uncertainty gave in to pain that went beyond her ability to do that. Didn't she deserve respect? Had she done something to make him think that he could take advantage of her mistake? How could she have thought he wouldn't be able to see her? She'd grown to trust him, but now she knew…she just couldn't.

The rain continued to pelt the ground, and the lightning and thunder sounded closer. The storm's fury matched the fury in her soul. As soon as she could, she was leaving. It wouldn't be soon enough since the damage was already done.

"Mercy?"

She didn't answer him. She didn't know how to put into words how broken she felt. She'd go with her original plan of starting over somewhere. Having money had its benefits. It wouldn't fix a broken heart, but she wouldn't be left on the side of the trail with no means.

She drew a deep shuddering breath and slowly let it out. The odor of burned beans filled the cave. She didn't care, let the pot be ruined. His shadow fell over her, and she quickly closed her eyes.

"Mercy, I know you're awake. What has you so upset, my love?" He squatted down in front of her.

She opened her eyes and pushed him backward. "Don't you dare call me your love. You treat me like some, some...*strumpet*. I know I'm not the ideal wife, and you're probably having second thoughts as we get closer to your home, but I do expect to be treated with respect."

His brow furrowed in confusion. "What are you talking about? Why would you think I'd consider you a strumpet?"

She sat up quickly. "I know you watched me when I got undressed. That's not how you treat a good woman." Once again her face heated.

He tilted his head and his frown disappeared. "I did look your way, and what I saw was so beautiful, I wanted to keep watching. I knew it wrong, and I turned away, but I couldn't help myself. I looked again and I looked my fill. You usually wear trousers and loose shirts, and to see your curves was pure joy. I'm sorry I upset you." A tender smile played on his lips. "I saw you looking at me."

"Yes I looked up, and that's how I found out just how much you'd seen. Now I'm going to sleep. Good night." She lay back down.

"It has been a long day." He took the pot out of the fire.

The next thing she knew, he placed his bedroll next to hers and spooned her with his arm draped over her middle.

Mercy held herself stiff. The turmoil in her heart was too much. She lay very still until she heard his light snoring. Then she relaxed and had to admit that being in his arms felt nice. She knew nothing about how a marriage worked. There was no one to ask but Greg. She always dreamed of being loved and cherished, but those were little-girl dreams.

Hardening her heart wouldn't work. It was as if he'd stolen her heart, but she felt the anguish of losing it. She'd have to hold on for at least another week. She couldn't stop the pain of loving him, but she'd put as much distance between them as she could. Keeping to herself should be easy enough.

For two days they'd been heading toward Oregon, and Greg was at his wits' end. Confound it! What was wrong with Mercy? She acted as though she hardly knew him. He'd thought they were getting closer than ever, and he'd hoped to have his wedding night. Had she changed her mind about being married?

She talked about living in town, when she did talk. It sounded like they wouldn't have a life on the ranch. He'd planned to build them a house. He was good with horses. Well, better than good. He'd been one of the best on the ranch beside his brother Juan. And he wanted her to meet Smitty and Lynn, his adopted parents.

He glanced at her riding up on the wagon seat, driving the team. He wanted nothing more than to pluck her off that seat and sit her in front of him so he could kiss her neck.

"Is something wrong?" Mercy didn't even look at him when she spoke.

"No, just admiring the view." He grinned when her face turned a rosy red. Perhaps there was a chance after all. He kept grinning until she finally scowled at him. Well maybe not. Either way, they needed to talk.

"I'm hoping we have nice weather the rest of the day. I

have an Uncle Jed who can predict when storms are coming and when they will be over. It came in handy on the Oregon Trail."

The day had been long, and anticipation began to fill him. They'd been on Settler land for about a mile. Should he tell Mercy? Maybe not. She might just ride in the other direction. He stopped them near a creek for the night. He wanted to get cleaned up. Mercy was off the wagon before he could even offer to help her down.

They tended the animals. Then after Greg started a fire. He grabbed the only clean clothes he had left, a bar of soap, and a towel, and headed to the creek. He made sure he was out of Mercy's view.

He undressed and dunked his whole body under the refreshing water. Making liberal use of the soap, he lathered his body, and immediately felt light of heart. He'd work things out with Mercy. He had to. After rinsing the soap off, he waded toward the bank and immediately saw that his clothes and towel were gone. Quickly, he scanned the area, but he didn't see anything out of place.

"Mercy! Very funny. Now can I have my clothes back?" He waited and there was no answer. "Mercy!"

She stomped toward him and her eyes widened. "Put some clothes on. This is not endearing you to me."

He grinned. "Very funny. Just give me my clothes back. I'm not mad, I just want to get dressed."

A frown graced her face, and his stomach dropped. "Run, get the guns!" He dropped down into the shallow water near the bank. He still didn't see anyone.

Mercy came running and dropped to the ground with gun in hand ready to shoot. She handed him both a towel and his sidearm. "I'll cover you while you get out of the creek. I don't have time to worry about your nakedness. Just get out of the water." She lay on her stomach looking for whoever was out there.

Greg ran toward Mercy without taking the time to cover up. Her eyes widened briefly, but then she quickly scanned the area. As soon as he had the towel wrapped around him, Mercy gestured with her head toward a clump of bushes.

Greg narrowed his eyes and waited. He stood up and walked out into the open. "Juan, come out before I blacken both of your eyes!"

There was laughter from the bushes.

"You too, Carlos. I swear you'll be sorry. You've scared my wife."

Two heads popped up. "Wife?" Juan asked.

"Yes, you two fools. This is Mercy, my wife." He helped Mercy up and grinned at the brothers.

"Mercy, these two jokesters are my brothers, Juan and Carlos. They were just about to apologize to you."

"Well I'll be dam… I mean it's a pleasure." Juan said. He took Mercy's hand and kissed it. Then he grinned at Greg.

"Nice to meet ya," Carlos said.

"Is it yours?" Juan asked.

Greg threw his gun down and took a swing at Juan. Juan ducked and threw his shoulder against Greg's legs, taking him down to the ground. First Juan had the advantage and got a good punch in. Blood spurted from Greg's lip. Greg immediately took control and was on top of Juan with his fist ready to hit his brother.

"Stop it, both of you!" Mercy shouted as she grabbed Greg's arm.

"Well, is it?" Carlos asked and Greg began to lunge at him but Mercy had a tight hold on him.

"She's not showing," Carlos said to Juan.

"What is wrong with you? I'm not in the family way! Why

we've never... Well, I'm just not, and I find it insulting." Mercy turned and stomped off toward the fire.

Greg shook his head at the other two. "Mercy is my wife. She deserves the respect due to her. She wasn't entirely sold on the idea of ranching, and you do this? You both should be ashamed of yourselves. I expect you to apologize to her."

Greg didn't feel much satisfaction at the sorry looks on their faces. He turned, grabbed his gun, and went to find Mercy.

She sat by the fire not looking at all upset. Puzzled, he sat next to her.

"I'm sorry about that."

"I'd appreciate it if you got dressed. Greg, I grew up with miners. There were fights daily, and I had to patch up my pa plenty of times."

Juan tossed Greg his clothes. Greg caught them and went behind some bushes to get dressed. He heard both boys apologize to Mercy and was relieved. He wouldn't have to try to hit them again. He wiped his lip with his hand and there was plenty of blood on the back when he pulled it away. How was he supposed to kiss Mercy now?

He came out from behind the bushes. He didn't expect to find a worried Mercy with clean water and a cloth to doctor him up. She grabbed his hand and sat him down. Her eyes looked soft and tender as she dabbed at his wound with the cloth. He didn't care if it hurt, just seeing her look at him that way was worth getting punched.

"What are you two doing all the way out here?" Greg asked.

"Juan has man pains and needs a place to get rid of them," Carlos said ruefully.

Greg glanced at Mercy and they both burst out laughing.

"What type of man pain can be fixed out here?" Greg

asked. He stopped laughing when he saw the hurt expression on Juan's face.

Juan shrugged. "I just want to be my own man. I want to be able to breed and train horses without constant yammering from Eli and Jed. Their way is the only way, and I'm tired of it. I'm old enough to be on my own."

Greg glanced from Juan to Carlos. They looked so much alike with their dark skin, black eyes, and long black hair. Greg had never known anyone that was Mexican before they became his new brothers. "What about Carlos? Pa won't like this, and Ma'll have a fit."

Juan smiled as though he already knew that, but it seemed to be news to Carlos, who scowled.

"I don't care. I'm staying with Juan!" Carlos jutted out his jaw.

Juan sighed. "So, how long have you two been hitched?"

Greg shrugged. "I think about three months?" He looked at Mercy for conformation.

"Three months and twelve days. It was right after my pa died." She stared into the fire.

Greg reached out and took her hand in his. Her hands might be small, but they did a powerful amount of work. He stroked her hand with his thumb. She shivered at his touch and his heart felt so much lighter.

"So Greg, you have a wife, but I bet you didn't find any gold like you planned. I knew you wouldn't find any," Carlos said.

Greg didn't correct him. "Mercy is my treasure." Her blush pleased him.

MERCY STARED AT THEM WISTFULLY. She'd always wanted brothers and sisters. "I can make some supper."

"No, I'm taking you to the creek so you can have a private bath. Juan is a great cook." Greg turned toward Juan. "You don't mind do you?"

"How long will this *bath* take? I'm starving." Carlos folded his arms in front of him.

She got up and grabbed clean clothes, along with her soap and a towel. "It'll take as long as it takes." She marched off toward the creek, not looking back. Greg would follow and make sure no one peeked. She stopped at the creek and hesitated. What about Greg? Would he think it his right to watch her? A lump formed in her throat.

Before she knew it, Greg was standing in front of her. He reached out and caressed her cheek. "I won't look. I never should have that night in the cave. You deserve my respect, and I knew you didn't want me to watch you. I've learned my lesson."

Nodding, she smiled. "I'll be quick. Carlos is hungry."

Greg laughed. "Don't let him fool you. He's always hungry." He turned his back.

She hesitated and decided she needed to trust him. She undressed and walked to the deepest part of the creek and dunked under the water. It felt delightful to have the mud and dust disappear. She lathered the soap in her hair, and when she finished rinsing herself she was in a better mood than she'd been in days.

"I'm coming out."

"Fine. It's getting cooler out. You might want to dress quickly."

He cared. She felt her splintered heart begin to mend. She dressed in record time. Of course she was wearing trousers and an oversized shirt. It would have been good to have something else to wear in front of his family, but she'd left her too-small, faded black dress behind.

"You can turn around now." The twinkle in his eyes had

her face heating, but she liked it. "Let's get to the fire so I can dry my hair." She began to walk, but Greg stood in place scowling. "What's wrong?"

"I don't want anyone but me to see your hair down. It's too beautiful to share."

"It's getting cold. I'm going to sit by the fire." Another splinter mended as she walked to the fire and sat down.

Greg reached into the trunk in the back of the wagon and brought her brush to her. She gave him what she hoped was one of her best smiles.

"Are we on your family's land already?" She wasn't sure she was ready to meet Greg's parents yet. Would they think her good enough to be their son's wife? She highly doubted it. She had never met anyone's standard of what a woman should be.

"Yes, the border is about a mile away. We jointly have a lot of land," Juan explained as he put a hoe cake on a plate and handed it to her.

"Thank you." She wished she was hungry, but her appetite had fled as her doubts crowded into her head. She was bound to be a disappointment. It was a good thing she planned to leave and start her own life.

Greg glanced at her. "Not hungry? That's not like you."

"I'm fine, really. It's been a long day is all." Pretending to be happy without a care in the world was exhausting. "Would it be rude if I spread out my bedroll?"

"Of course not." Greg took her plate from her and grabbed her bedroll from the back of the wagon. He placed it close to the fire. He looked worried, and that made her feel guilty.

She lay down and turned her back to them. They talked in low voices, and soon she drifted off.

CHAPTER NINE

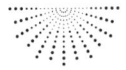

The house was in sight, and Mercy could feel Greg's excitement, in vast contrast to the dread that filled her. She couldn't stop the thoughts in her head that said she wasn't worthy and they would hate her.

She was used to the rough and tumble life of the gold mines. She was sure to embarrass Greg. He was such a good man, and he deserved better. Juan and Carlos gave their horses their heads and off they went. If not for the heavy gold they were hauling Greg probably would have followed.

Taking off her hat, she tried to smooth down her hair. It hung down her back and when she tried to rake her fingers through it, she noted just how knotted it was.

"I can't go." She reined in the team.

Greg stopped right next to her. "Why not?" His brow furrowed as he frowned.

"Look at me. I don't dress like a woman, and my hair is a mess, and your family will think you married some street urchin. I know how nice women look at me. I've seen it when I went into stores with my pa. Just point me in the direction of the nearest town." Tears filled her eyes.

"No."

Her breath left her in a whoosh. "No? Why not? You couldn't possibly want to be saddled with me."

Greg grinned. "Perhaps I do want to be saddled with you, Mercy Settler. No one will look down at you. They'll be happy that I made a good choice in a bride. I know I'm happy." He stared into her eyes, and she saw the truth of his words.

She nodded and urged the team on. Her hands shook slightly as she drove the wagon to the house. Greg jumped down and was at her side. He helped her down and took her hand, giving it a gentle squeeze.

A pretty young girl walked out the door, took one look at Mercy, and shook her head. "Certainly this isn't—"

"Scarlett, this is my wife Mercy."

"Nice to meet you," Mercy said. Her heart sank when Scarlett shook her perfect head with her perfect dark hair. She turned around in her beautiful green dress and rushed back inside.

Mercy took her hand back. "I'll get going now." She hated how pitiful her voice sounded.

The next thing she knew so many people piled out of the house, she had no idea how they had all fit inside. An older woman smiled at her then walked up and hugged her. "Welcome, Mercy. Juan and Carlos were just singing your praises. My name is Lynn, and I'm Greg's ma." She turned to Greg and there were tears in her eyes when she hugged him tight to her. "I'm so glad you're back."

Greg hugged her just as tight. "It's good to be back, Ma."

Lynn Settler stepped back and looked him over. "Definitely a man now."

Greg turned red. "Ma, you can't say things like that."

Lynn laughed. "Come on into the house, both of you."

Greg reached out, grasped Mercy's hand, and led her to

the house. Once they were inside, she could see the house was unusually large. The table in the kitchen was as long as the tables in the mining camp.

"How many kids live here?"

Lynn poured coffee into three mugs. "Well, we have Juan, Carlos, Scarlett, Cindy, Brian, Will, Oscar, Alex, and Rose. And since you've been gone, Greg, we have added Hunter, Anthony, Jax, Mia, and Cotton. Sit, let's have coffee."

The three of them sat down, and then a young boy came bounding in. "Greg you're back! Did you strike it rich?"

Greg smiled back. "I sure did and her name is Mercy." He grinned at her. "Mercy, this is my brother Will."

Will frowned. "Howdy, Ma'am. I was thinking about gold."

"That too. Some's on the mule. The rest is buried in the wagon. Will you help bring it all in the house?"

"Sure thing, Greg," Will yelled as he ran out the front door.

The big house, meeting Greg's ma, the number of orphans... It all overwhelmed Mercy. Not only did she know she looked ugly and plain, she wasn't used to family life. She was bound to make herself appear awful. She didn't know how to deal with his family. How would she remember their names? She felt the blood drain from her face. Now she must look pasty white.

"How did you two meet?" Lynn asked.

"I covered him with my shotgun while he was being shot at," answered Mercy. "He got to safety."

Lynn's eyes widened. "At the gold mines? Mercy, you were there?"

"Yes, ma'am. I grew up in the mines. Me and my pa, we traveled from claim to claim. It's not such a bad life. We had each other until he was shot in his own mine. It was a bad time. Greg almost got hanged for it, but I knew the judge. He insisted we marry. Greg and I became partners, and we'd fight about the perfume on him when he came back to the mine with it on his clothes." She took a deep breath. Why couldn't she seem to stop chattering?

Lynn cocked her left brow. "Perfume?"

Greg narrowed his eyes when he glanced at Mercy. "I had to go to the saloon to see what was going on is all. We barely got out of there with our lives and the gold." He shrugged. "Now I have a wife."

He didn't sound very cheerful about the wife part, and Mercy allowed her shoulders to sag. Perhaps it would be best to just be quiet.

Two girls came running into the kitchen giggling and then they stopped.

"I thought Scarlett was fibbing," the blond girl said.

"I never had much but I always had a dress. I never had to dress like a man," the girl with light brown hair said.

The blood quickly returned to Mercy's face and she grew hot.

"Girls," Lynn said in a disapproving voice. "Mercy, this is Cynthia and Mia."

Cynthia was the blond and she barely gave Mercy a nod.

Mia didn't even look embarrassed by her words. "Don't you have a dress?"

"Mia, I think that is quite enough. Come meet your brother Greg."

Mia scowled at Lynn and then she smiled sweetly at Greg. "I've heard so much about you, Greg. Everyone is right. You are very handsome."

"Girls, why don't you go tell your pa that Greg is back," Lynn suggested. She appeared relieved when they ran out the door.

"Mercy, I'm so sorry. Cynthia was very shy until Mia

GREG

came to live with us." She hesitated. "Perhaps Greg can get your things and you can change." Lynn's voice was gentle.

Mercy stood and nodded. "I can get my own things." She hurried outside and was relieved to see the saddlebags had not been unloaded from Greg's horse.

She quickly mounted and rode the way they'd come. Her pride had taken quite a beating. Between her heart breaking and her pride being ripped to shreds, she wasn't sure which hurt more. Her father must have protected her from people like Cynthia and Mia. She couldn't ride into town. It was Greg's town, and she didn't want to embarrass him. She still had her gold flake and nuggets in Greg's saddlebags. She'd survive.

GREG PUSHED BACK his chair hard as he stood. He's been sorely disappointed by his sisters' reaction to Mercy. "I have to go get my wife. She thought she'd be judged here because of her lack of clothes and because her hair, though clean, wasn't styled in any fashion." Bitterness he couldn't control colored his words. "I assured her everyone here was kind and it wouldn't matter. They'd see past those things and realize how nice she was. I'll be back."

Before his ma could say a word, he left. Will, Juan, and Carlos all stared at him as he quickly saddled another horse from the barn and mounted. Juan pointed in the direction Mercy had gone, and Greg nodded his thanks.

GREG HAD BEEN RIDING for at least an hour. Where was she? She didn't have much of a lead on him. But he couldn't see any trail that she'd left. He heard a horse coming up behind him and grabbed his gun, turning his horse. Relief swept through him. He wanted to tear up at the sight of Smitty, his pa.

"Which way?" Smitty asked.

"I lost her, I think. She can handle herself outdoors."

"Did you see any tracks at all?"

"Yes, before the woods, and then they vanished." He shook his head, overcome by sadness. "She probably won't come back with me anyway."

Smitty stared at him. "I thought you two were married."

"We were forced to get married, and we've been trying to find our way, but it never works out." A sigh slipped out. "I haven't even had my wedding night. She can be as prickly as a cactus."

"Do you love her?"

"Yes, I do."

Smitty sighed. "Does she know that?"

Greg shook his head. "I don't know." He swallowed hard.

Smitty turned his horse. "Put the gun away, and let's go to the last point you saw tracks."

Greg watched his pa ride off. He quickly put his gun in its holster and followed. When they got to the edge of the woods, Greg took the lead. He reined his horse in and jumped down.

Smitty was soon beside him. He squatted down and looked in all directions. "She went through the forest." He cursed under his breath. "Women never go the easy way. She won't get anywhere fast. She'll need to lead her horse through the underbrush."

The held their horses' reins and walked into the woods.

"Pa, what difference does a dress make? Mercy is a kind woman, and she's very hard working. She was worried about how she looked, but I assured her everyone would be nice."

"Lynn said she grew up mining? The house and all the kids probably made her nervous, so any comments about what she was wearing were too much for her. Lynn said she's beautiful."

"That she is. And she has a kind heart. She knows everything about mining, and she taught me a lot. She saved my bacon more than once. She's the type of woman I could build a life with. I wanted to build a house of our own here on the ranch."

"Did she know your plans?"

He nodded. "We talked about it."

Smitty stopped and listened. "She's by the stream to the left. Go get your wife. You can live in my old house for now, and I'll have Lynn leave a few dresses and woman things there for her. Take meals with us when you can. You have many new brothers and a sister you haven't met. The house is near bursting and your ma and I have never been happier. Good luck. Oh, and Greg, I'm so glad you came home." He turned his horse and headed for the house.

His pa's words warmed him. He led his horse toward the creek. He made enough noise so Mercy wouldn't get jumpy and shoot him if he snuck up on her. "Mercy, are you there?"

She didn't answer, but he heard a sob and his heart squeezed. He walked faster, then let go of the reins. Her head was bowed as she sat on a fallen log near the creek. The horse was nearby, grazing. He sat next to her and she didn't even glance at him. Greg put his hand under her chin and turned her face toward him.

Her red eyes had a look of defeat in them and he'd never seen Mercy look defeated. He caught a tear with his thumb, but he wasn't able to keep up with the flood of tears that poured down her face. Immediately, he pulled her into his arms and held her tight as she sobbed against his shirt.

His whole being wanted to cry for the pain she was experiencing. He'd known she was nervous about meeting his family but he hadn't realized how vulnerable she was. He'd like to take a paddle to his sisters, including the new one. Mia was her name? His ma was so kind and gentle. Why couldn't they learn to be that way too?

He stroked her back and his gut hurt with every sob. Maybe they should have stayed at the mine. No, it was too dangerous. She was where she belonged, with him.

"Mercy, I'm so sorry. They're young and didn't mean to make you feel uncomfortable."

She pulled away and blinked. "You were there. Didn't you see the gleam in their eyes that accompanied their words? I don't belong here. Your house is so big, and I'm nothing but a miner."

"You are my wife. We'll work through this."

She shook her head. "What's to work through? They looked at me and found me lacking. It doesn't get any better from there. I want to go my own way. I should have stuck to my original plan."

His heart dropped. "No."

"What do you mean no? This is my life we're talking about! I don't plan to live it being ridiculed. I might look tough but sometimes my heart is too tender for its own good. I usually just chalk up insults to the ignorance of the miner who said it."

He still had her in the circle of his arms, afraid to let go. She might make a run for it. "I need you. I want you here. You're my wife."

"Not really."

"Yes, in every way that counts. I love you, Mercy Settler, and I'm not going to let you go. You're an amazing woman, and I want you by my side building a future for us. We have a house to build, and I'm sure we'll want a vegetable garden, and we can raise the best horses. I was also hoping we'd have a family of our own. You'd be a wonderful mother."

"I don't know the first thing about raising children. I'll

make a mess of it." She turned her head and laid it on his shoulder. "We had our time together, and we got our gold. I'm going to go to one town and buy clothes and practice being a proper lady, and then I'm going to another town to live. I want to start over in a place where I feel wanted."

"Have you heard a word I've been saying? I love you!"

She stiffened for a moment and then pulled away from him. Then she stared into his eyes. "You don't mean that."

"Mercy, I mean it from the depths of my soul." He leaned in and kissed her. It was a sweet, tender kiss at first, but then it deepened and her body relaxed against him. She wrapped her arms around his neck pulling him as close as possible. Then she pushed him away, got up and mounted the horse again, and before he knew it, she was riding down the middle of the creek bed.

He watched her go, taking his heart with her. Tears filled his eyes as pain rushed through him. He'd given her his love, and she didn't want it. A sense of grief overwhelmed him, and he wasn't sure what to do next.

He sat on the log hoping with everything inside him that she'd come back, but as the sun began to go down, his hopes and dreams shattered. Finally he led his horse out of the dense woods and rode home.

His pa sat on the front porch in a rocking chair, probably one he'd made, smoking his pipe. Will took the horse and Greg walked up the porch steps. He slumped down into a chair and closed his eyes. He wished he could scream and yell until his hurt went away, but he didn't think it would ever go away.

"She wouldn't come back?" His pa's voice was gentle and understanding.

"I told her I love her, and she left anyway. She didn't think she could fit in here." He shook his head. "Pa, we're all a band of misfits, and you and Ma made us into a family. I knew she could be a bit prickly, but I didn't realize how vulnerable she was. I'm not sure what I'll do without her."

"I'm sorry it played out that way, son. My offer to stay at my old cabin stands."

His ma rushed out the front door and an expression of dismay crossed her face. "She left?"

Greg had such a lump in his throat, he couldn't answer.

"Mercy went her own way. Greg will be using my old cabin for a while." Smitty took Lynn's hand and kissed the back of it.

"Let me get you a plate of food to take with you. I'll have Juan bring your things to you. Greg, I'm so sorry. She seemed like a good match for you."

Greg just nodded. He wasn't hungry. He walked down the steps and to the cabin. Being alone would be better than dealing with all the questions he was sure his brothers and sisters would ask.

CHAPTER TEN

Mercy shivered, although she sat by a roaring fire. She'd be fine, just fine. Who needed a husband? Her eyes ached from crying. Why hadn't she found out where the towns were located before she stormed off? How stupid! She didn't have any supplies, just a bit of gold. Gold wasn't worth anything out in the wilderness.

Her pride still smarted from Greg's sisters. For some reason, she thought since they were all orphans they'd be more welcoming. Lynn was nice, and she could tell that was where Greg got his kindness.

In the distance, she heard a bobcat growl. Her fire was plenty big to keep all the wild creatures away. And she had her gun but no bedroll. It had been almost impossible to tell what direction she'd been going in the dense woods. Perhaps she'd be able to see what direction the morning sunrise was. She probably needed to go east.

Drawing her legs up, she rested her head on her knees. Greg said he loved her. He wouldn't lie about that. She was positive. It warmed her a bit, but it made her heart ache all the more. Sure, she could buy new clothes, but she didn't know much beyond mining and the outdoors. Certainly nothing about being a wife or…a mother. Sighing loudly, she decided to get out of the woods tomorrow. Then she'd know in what direction she was going.

It was lonely without Greg. He'd been a real gentleman and he cared for her. She loved him too. She heard the bobcat again but it was still far away. She'd get no sleep that night.

It came down to her pride, and she shook her head. If she recalled her Bible correctly, it said, *When pride comes, then comes disgrace, but with humility comes wisdom.* There was another verse if she could only remember it. She sat up and stared into the flames. *Where there is strife, there is pride, but wisdom is found in those who take advice.*

SHE PONDERED the Bible verses for a while. She really hadn't given Greg's family a chance. There were so many of them, and she'd probably only met a few. Did it really matter what they thought? She was a good person, and she was willing to learn and take advice. Her pride had gotten in her way. Would Greg want her back?

He was probably hurting too. She never meant for him to say he loved her without her telling him she loved him back. She'd made so many mistakes. She could probably find her way back but then what? They needed to talk when she wasn't crying. His family probably now thought even less of her for leaving.

She thought long and hard all night, and as the sun rose, she'd made her decision. She'd go back. She could barely make out in which direction the sun was rising but she could see enough. She could tell where the sky was lightening. She'd have to forget about her pride and listen to what Greg had to say with an open heart. It was the right thing to do.

GREG

She found the creek and followed it out of the woods and then mounted the horse. She rode in the direction of Greg's home. Butterflies fluttered in her stomach as she rode. Eventually, the house was in sight, and she reined in the horse. Her hands shook a bit as she took a deep breath. What if he'd decided he didn't want her anymore? She dug deep inside of herself and gathered her courage.

Pulling her hat down, she hoped her eyes wouldn't look too puffy and red. The horse kept to a slow walk as she approached. There were many people in the yard doing various things, laundry, tending the garden, and snapping beans. There was no sign of Greg. Everything within her wanted to turn around, but Greg deserved better.

A large man with thick dark hair smiled widely at her. He walked to her and plucked her out of the saddle. He gave her a big hug. It was the type of hug that could heal one's soul.

"Welcome home, Mercy. I'm Greg's pa, Smitty. Everything will be fine," he whispered in her ear as he held her.

He took the horse's reins in one hand and her hand in the other, and they walked on by the big house. They came to a log cabin, and Smitty tied the horse to the hitching post. Then he turned to Mercy and gave her another hug. "I'm glad my son has you. Now go and knock on the door. Tell him Lynn will send food down so you two can have privacy for a few days." He lightly squeezed her shoulder and walked away.

The door was her last barrier to Greg, and she needed to knock on it, but part of her was terrified to do so. She took a few steps, and the wooden door flew open. Greg stood there looking as though he'd not slept either. *What does a person say in this situation?*

"Mercy?" He held her gaze as he walked to her. Then he smiled and gathered her into his embrace, twirling her around until she laughed.

He put her down. "I thought I lost you. It was the worst night of my life, wondering if you were safe."

She took a big breath and let it out. "Greg, I love you too, with all my heart and soul. I'm ashamed I didn't tell you sooner."

The love he felt reflected in his eyes.

"I don't know if I'll be a good wife to you. There is so much I don't know about ranching."

"I didn't know anything about mining, yet you made a fine gold miner out of me. I can teach you anything you need to know. You're smart, and you're a hard worker." His grin widened. "And you're nice to look at."

She swatted his arm. "I don't look so good this morning."

Greg took her hand and led her to the cabin's doorway. He lifted her into his arms and carried her over the threshold. When he put her down, he gave her a kiss so tender she wanted to cry all over again. He led her to the bed, and her nerves began to get the better of her.

He kissed her again. It was a nice, long kiss. It felt as though he put his love in the kiss. He then sat her on the bed and took off her jacket and shoes. "There's a clean night gown for you. You get some sleep."

"You need sleep too."

"I'll come to bed in a bit. Don't worry we can go slow. Right now we both need sleep."

He was such a special man. She smiled and nodded. "I didn't feel whole without you."

Greg nodded. "Same here." He closed the door behind him.

Taking off her hat, she then shook out her long tresses and picked up the nightgown. It was made of white muslin with a pink bow at the neck line. There was even a bit of lace around the sleeves. It was the prettiest thing she'd ever seen.

GREG

She hurriedly undressed and put it on. It was so soft against her skin.

Next, she pulled back the quilt and there were sheets on the bed. She didn't know the last time she'd slept between sheets. Eagerly, she hopped into bed and placed her head on the plump pillow.

After a moment, the bed jostled, and she realized that Greg was getting in next to her. He spooned behind her and put his arm around her waist. His light snore was soothing, and she soon fell asleep.

Greg propped himself up on his elbows and stared down at his sleeping wife. He thanked God for his good fortune. His heart near exploded, it was so full of love. He really hadn't thought she was going to come back. He was admiring her long hair when her green eyes opened.

Her smile was one of a peaceful heart. It was so different from when she first got here. Reaching out, he stroked her hair and then caressed her cheek.

Mercy reached up and pulled his head down for a kiss. He was trying to figure out if they should consummate the marriage or wait, but the ardor of her kiss gave him the direction he needed.

"I'll be gentle," he murmured.

"I know you will and I want to be yours for all time."

He kissed her neck and was delighted when she shivered. Then he helped her take her gown off. "You are beautiful, Mercy." He laughed as her skin began to turn red.

She wrapped her arms around his neck, and he needed no more encouragement. He made her his wife as gently as he could.

When they were done, she stared at him as if in wonder. It had been so much better than he imagined.

"Are you all right?" he asked.

She nodded and grinned. "I'm more than all right, Greg. I'm your wife now, and it was beautiful."

He kissed her again and settled on his back bringing her with him so she could lay her head on his chest. Once again they slept.

EPILOGUE

Tables were laden with an enormous amount of food. The Settlers and the Todds were all celebrating the new house. With so many people, Greg figured the food would be gone soon and then the dancing would start. It was a noisy affair.

Greg held Mercy's hand as they walked a bit and then gazed upon their completed house. So many people had helped build it. The best part was, Mercy had felt welcomed and part of the family now. No one else cared what she wore, but she now wore the ready-made dresses that Greg had bought for her. He'd take her to town in a few days so she could visit the new dressmaker there.

He'd given her a choice of what to wear, and she wanted dresses. She looked so beautiful and feminine in them. She'd amazed them all by climbing to the top of the house to help with the roof. She'd smiled when she saw the admiration in his sisters' eyes.

He stared at her profile, his heart full of love. They had amassed a fortune in gold, but she still liked simple things. They could have ordered so many fancy things for the house, but she was a tin plate, flour-sack kind of woman. He'd offered money to his ma and pa, but they refused it. So, he'd set it aside. Who knew what would happen if they kept taking in more orphans? They'd need money to clothe them all.

"Next is the barn and corral?" Mercy asked.

"Yes, a strictly horse barn and the corral will be big enough to train horses. The best thing is Juan and I won't step on Eli and Jed's toes. The Calvary wants as many horses as we can provide."

"You did this for Juan," she remarked softly.

"Yes, I was afraid he'd leave and get himself in trouble. I don't understand the tension between him and Eli and Jed. Especially Jed. They've known him since they joined our family. He was the leader of the wagon train we were on."

"This way Carlos won't run away trying to find his brother. You're a good man Greg Settler." Mercy smiled at him. She reached up and stroked his beard.

"It was the best day of my life when you came back to me. You are the love of my life." Greg took her into his arms and kissed her soundly. "Maybe we can bathe under that waterfall over yonder."

Mercy blushed. "It's a date."

"I think we ended up with the best piece of land and truthfully I was amazed that the land was still available. I had to wait until I was eighteen, but I got our 640 acres of free land."

"You're so impatient!" She laughed. "You didn't have a long wait. Your birthday was a month after we got here. I've never seen such a celebration! Did I mention my birthday is in six weeks?" Her laugh faded to a secretive smile. "But I'd rather have a private birthday with just you. This time next year we won't have any privacy."

GREG

Greg shrugged. "Juan will build his house far enough away so we won't have to worry."

"That's good. I wouldn't want crying to wake him or anything."

Greg furrowed his brow. "Sweetheart, I don't ever expect to make you cry."

Mercy laughed again. "I never thought you could be so dense."

He stared at her. "Just tell me what you mean."

Her smile deepened. "I'm with child."

"What?" Greg immediately picked her up and spun her around. "Yee Haw!"

"Put me down! You're making me sick!"

Greg instantly stopped and put her back on her feet. "Are you all right? What about the baby? I didn't make the baby dizzy did I?"

Smitty and Lynn had walked their way. Smitty roared with laughter. "Greg, I guess I need to explain babies to you," He said in between guffaws.

Lynn hugged Mercy for a good, long time. "I'm so happy for you both!"

Smitty took his turn hugging Mercy. "You make sure my son is good to you. No more climbing up to the roof for you, young lady."

Greg's mouth dropped open. "Were you with child when you were building the house?"

Mercy smiled and shrugged. "If I had told you, then you would have made me sit and watch. I'm not one to sit and watch, you know."

"I can see I'll have my hands full with you, my love."

Mercy walked into the circle of his arms. "For always."

THE END

I'm so pleased you chose to read Greg, and it's my sincere hope that you enjoyed the story. I would appreciate if you'd consider posting a review. This can help an author tremendously in obtaining a readership. My many thanks. ~ Kathleen

ABOUT THE AUTHOR

Sexy Cowboys and the Women Who Love Them...
Finalist in the 2012 and 2015 RONE Awards.
Top Pick, Five Star Series from the Romance Review.
Kathleen Ball writes contemporary and historical western romance with great emotion and
memorable characters. Her books are award winners and have appeared on best sellers lists including: Amazon's Best Seller's List, All Romance Ebooks, Bookstrand, Desert Breeze Publishing and Secret Cravings Publishing Best Sellers list. She is the recipient of eight Editor's Choice Awards, and The Readers' Choice Award for Ryelee's Cowboy.
Winner of the Lear diamond award Best Historical Novel- Cinders' Bride
There's something about a cowboy

facebook.com/kathleenballwesternromance

twitter.com/kballauthor

instagram.com/author_kathleenball

OTHER BOOKS BY KATHLEEN

Lasso Spring's Series

Callie's Heart

Lone Star Joy

Stetson's Storm

Dawson Ranch Series

Texas Haven

Ryelee's Cowboy

Cowboy Season Series

Summer's Desire

Autumn's Hope

Winter's Embrace

Spring's Delight

Mail Order Brides of Texas

Cinders' Bride

Keegan's Bride

Shane's Bride

Tramp's Bride

Poor Boy's Christmas

Oregon Trail Dreamin' ✓

We've Only Just Begun

A Lifetime to Share

A Love Worth Searching For

So Many Roads to Choose

The Settlers

Greg ✓

Juan ✓ 2

The Greatest Gift

Love So Deep ✓

Luke's Fate ✓

Whispered Love ✓

Love Before Midnight

I'm Forever Yours ✓

Finn's Fortune ✓

Made in the USA
San Bernardino, CA
27 September 2018